WHERE TYNDRA TURNS TO ARDNYT

The first of the Norn Novellas

A. NICKY HJORT

Lavish
Publishing LLC

First Edition

The Norn Novella Series book 1

All Rights Reserved

Published in the United States by Lavish Publishing, LLC, Midland, Texas

Paperback edition

ISBN:9781944985189

Cover Design by: Wycked Ink

Cover Images: Adobe Stock

www.LavishPublishing.com

Contents

To Marsha, my Mom, who is Love's First Kiss.

Prologue

ZA, the least known, yet most intriguing of the four immortal Norn Sisters, hid crying in her family's empty tomb. If she had a mother or father to speak of, she would have run to them for advice, but alas...the only limited guidance offered her during crisis came from Odin, ruler of her universe. Since He was always too busy creating this or destroying that, He never bothered to answer her questions satisfactorily. Thus, the clever, but devastated, creature sought solace in the only thing she knew for suremagic.

She remembered the horrible image that had driven her to such despair, and she wailed. Enhrik, the demigod she loved as much as her fickle heart would ever allow her to love anything, had delivered up her eldest sister's body as a sacrificial feast on the table of a monstrous beast, the Enfield, a mutant with mixed parts of multiple creatures: a wolf's face, the wings and talons of an eagle, and a fox's tail all on the body of a lion that loved to eat little children.

But why?

Probably because a Norn's sempiternal blood would prolong the monster's disgusting existence. Everybody knew that. *Or, oh no!* Maybe the demon planned to do unthinkable things to the sister's flawless body to quench his insatiable lust.

Oh what an idiot she had been to trust that charming demigod. Did Enhrik not realize Za would discover such an evil plot against her and the other Sisters of Norn? How many times had she been here like thisfooled and unable to make wise choices? Too many times to count. This time, she would show him yet!

She would curse them all.

Whilst her tears dripped across the marble floor beneath her fragile feet, Za lost all track of time in her suffering and slipped perilously into an altered state where she could work her darker forms of magic. She damned the ugly beast that had planned to consume her sister using her most terrible powers to entangle him a wall of ivy as thick as his unbearable face was awful. If the last leaf of the magical ivy shriveled and died, she vowed the beast should perish with it.

Who knew, other than Odin, how many eons passed while she schemed her terrible schemes, locking up her own memory of the event in the process? Had her sister survived the blood letting? Would the monster escape his prison of ivy? Would her lover even miss her, even try to find her, even try to undo what he had done?

She wanted to know, but wanted *not* to know even more.

Her will split right down the middle, her inner truth divided in two.

So as to selfishly compound the effects of her misery, Za took her retribution one cruel step further. She pulled Odin's snow globe out of her pocket and wiped her face dry. The snow globeOdin's most prized possessiongone by her doing, stolen in her fit of rage against her God. The same God who never once directly answered her pleas for help or acted like the parent she so terribly craved. But worst of all, for allowing her lover to destroy her world and violate everything she ever knew as good or valuable to appease such an ugly enemy.

How dare Odin treat her this way! She would show Him yet.

Even through her drops of salty outpour, the wildly spirited and somewhat self-centered Norn giggled nervously with pleasure at her clever plot. Bringing the notorious artifact with her to punish her Creator was most definitely brilliant. Her most wicked scheme so far, in fact, to take from Him the one thing he loved so unconditionally. Well damn the worthless globe, then.

Helplessly terrified and excited to be so close to something so fine and frail that had always warranted so much of His majesty's focus, *unlike her*, she gulped down the limited air in this locked space and held on to it so tightly her chest ached from the effort. Eyes wide with jealous fascination and hands that shook with fearful anticipation, she peered into the glass with mounting trepidation at what pain this indulgence of revenge and hatred might cost her in the end.

Odin would be devastated from its loss.

Perhaps He would destroy the universe to punish her. She smiled. Perhaps He would destroy the universe to teach her a lesson. She snickered.

Oh how it drove her mad the way He always held this globe so close to His lips with such devotion, such joy, such quiet reverence, and not infrequently, such forlorn grief as if He were blowing it a kiss. It was as if this stupid ball of glass contained a miniature version of everything that had ever mattered to Himthe prime creator, caller of life, breather of love. Since it was love's fault her heart was so broken, after all, she felt justified in her revengeful plot against Himthe source of all the love in the world.

The tiniest of the Norns brought Odin's snow globe closer to her face, now closer still, now so close it filled her entire measure of vision and consumed all the fragments of her splintered focus into one great stream of powerful intention.

Oh how instantly she was enraptured with this intriguing little worldso naïve, so oblivious to its doom because of the whim of a Norn in the greater world outside the thick glass wall that enclosed it.

Immediately, she felt with absolute certainty she belonged inside the glass, and so she wished to be a human until the end of tyme. Of course, the dear child knew that so very insignificant desire was ridiculous, but observing this treasure seemed like a much more interesting and deadly game to play…one where even she might discover something new and terrible.

For a moment, she considered it might have been Odin's will that she found the priceless globe to begin withunprotected and out in the open like she had.

But that was silly. Or was it?

Suddenly, she wondered why she hadn't stolen the globe before now and laughed nervously at her treachery. Even though she knew she *shouldn't* take such liberty with something so innocent, part of her knew she *must.* Like a magnet, hidden deep within her heart and so much more powerful than all the *shoulds or shouldn'ts* combined, that undeniable allure drew her hand onto the ball and closed her fine, magical fingers around it.

Must. I simply, must.

Even she couldn't have stopped herself if she had wanted to.

Besides, she had already taken it. There was no putting it back now.

She couldn't be sure if anyone had seen her enter the tomb with the globe, but she thought not. Chest heaving and short of breath, she examined the globe again.

First, she read the minute inscription on the column running down the center from right-to-left, then from left-to-right, not able to see much of a difference, other than the order of the letters. Was there a difference between the two simple names if they contained all the same letters?

She took her inquiry one step further; could up and down, forward and backward, alive and dead, love and hate, all or nothing really be the same things, just in a different order, too?

Perhaps. Perhaps not.

The magnet within her soul took her interesting question yet another dangerous step forward and pushed her to action; she shook the invaluable ball of glass, tossing the contents in every direction at once. With one forceful, yet final shake of her wrist and intention, she split the precious little existence into two halves and laid the globe down on its side. The ultimate duality—all the good things fell to one side, all the bad things fell to the other.

She peered deep within the thick glass, so deeply she lost both parts of her splintered will to it—both the *must* know part of her and *must not* know part of her.

Was it years? Was it days? Was it eons? Or was it only one breath that the little Norn stayed inside the glass prison of her own making before this story played out? Just what exactly was she trying so desperately to teach herself by doing such a silly thing and wasting so much tyme?

Who, other than Odin, could have possibly known?

Section I: In Tyndra

Are we not drawn onward, drawn onward to new era?

Sore was I ere I saw Eros.
 Never a foot too far, even,

Draw, O Caesar, erase a coward.

Red Roses run no risk, sir, on nurses' order.
 Eve damned Eden, mad Eve.
 Live not on evil deed, live not on evil.

No word, no bond, row on.

"Revolt, love!" raved Eva. "Revolt, lover!"
 Rise, sir lapdog! Revolt, lover! God, pal, rise, sir!

Live on, Time; emit no evil.
 Now Eve, we're here, we've won,
 Madam, I'm Adam.

Are we not drawn onward, drawn onward to new era?

- The Irminsul of Tyndra

Chapter One

TIRED BY THE thought of even getting out of bed this morning, nineteen-year-old Azza, last of the Ivi daughters, yawned and then moaned, desperately trying to drag back a second more of her precious reoccurring dream. The sparkle of her hair in the vision, indescribably brighter than the color of the sun at its most intense moment on its least cloudy day, pleased her beyond measure.

The young boy's eyes in her visiona shade so deep, so rich they contained colors within colors she had no name for but imagined must exist somewhere on the other side of the sky's heavy and dreary clouds. Like every morning before this one, his hungry eyes slipped perilously away before her warm breath had escaped her chapped lips. Starving for the texture of his body, she reached up to stroke the boy's neck and experience the burn of the hot and inviting mark that defined him even more than those delicious eyes: a diamond-shaped scar that glowed crimson. Oh how hot it pulsed, fiery and more determined than the last ember in the pits to burn eternally, just beneath the nape of his muscular neck. But painfully, the once-flaming image was already small and dark, too small and insignificant to hold on to.

Then it was just gone like frozen milk cubes that have shattered on a dirty stone floor and are wasted beyond reprieve.

Talby, an assuming and greedy baby fox, scurried across the room to greet Azza, and the simple girl smiled despite her sadness from the stolen dream. Briefly, she tried to bring it back for one fractured moment longer, but to no avail, thus, offered her attention to the creature instead.

The hungry fox cried out, demanding Azza feed it something, anythingpreferably warm milk.

"Well, at least you are predictable, Talby. Gone all night to who knows where and back just in tyme for breakfast." She shook her finger at the animal, and he wagged his tail to the rhythm of her hand. She laughed and would have sworn he laughed, too.

One month prior, she had rescued the poor creature still suckling on his mother's dead teat, obviously shot in case she was one of the infamous Enfield's pack of mutant wolf-like servants. As if the Enfield was something more than a made up beast in a made up story invented to scare away the curious little children from playing too near the Ivy Wall. What kind of idiot didn't recognize the beauty and much smaller size of a red fox as compared to a red monster that didn't even exist?

Red, the color so intense and gorgeous, such a rarity in this kingdom.

What did those stupid legends have against red anyway? Like the myth of the red wolf that ate little girls in red capes. Total absurditynothing more than a horrified fairytale written by some fools named Grimm. Grimm so grim.

Unlike most of the illiterate villagers in Tyndra, the cold and barren land she called home, Azza had read the stories that her people took to be truth. Fairytales were turned by fear into vehicles to grow more fear: a vicious and cruel cycle that sucked the life out of her people. The problem always seemed to grow because fear blocked the way to the only possible answer to the riddle. And the cure? Overwhelming gratitude, of course.

The soldier who shot Talby's mother was an idiot, and the only thing more dangerous than an idiot was a fearful idiot with a deadly weapon. The fool could have as easily shot the children he was supposed to be out protecting. The same little darlings murdered by the soldiers trying to stop whatever kept going on around here. *Awful.*

Even Azza had to admit children had disappeared. Always missing, without a trace, never to be found again.

Maybe the little girl in the red cape had eaten them, not the wolf at all. She laughed at the idea of turning the tale on its head and spinning it round the other way, but the thought drug her back down to reality. *Children missing.*

She tried to remember the count so far—at least three, maybe four.

However, lost was better than found—found chewed and partially digested by an evil Red Riding Hood on her way to grandmother's house, but found nonetheless. It seemed to Azza, *not found* was much better than *found* dead. *Thank Odin for the not found babies.*

Azza knew gratitude was the cure for every fear, so she decided to offer up some more of that instead. Thanks to Odin, Talby had been a crafty and natural survivor unlike his four brothers, Azza had a scrap left to feed him, the last baby was still missing and *not found*, and she had survived her birth even though her mother hadn't.

Talby mewed; clearly he agreed with Azza's thought process. Or maybe he was just adding his gratitude for the morsel of food.

"I'm sorry, Talby. Everyone needs a mama. Even me. I'll be your mama, and you can be mine. Deal?"

Pets were now forbidden to the general population after the last child, the youngest daughter of Tyndra's chief of masonry, had gone missing from her own bedroom in the middle of the night, four nights prior.

Azza never liked that manswollen nose, sunken and blood-shot eyes from drinking too much Meade. The kind of eyes that hid rather well under a red cape, now she thought about it. Perhaps it was his fault. Perhaps he was Little Red in disguise. Perhaps he had eaten the wolf instead of the other way around.

The made-up mutated wolves, always accused of dirty deeds on behalf of their evil master, the Enfieldthe imaginary antithesis of the benevolent Odinwere blamed for this tragedy like they were blamed for the lack of fresh deer meet, squirrels, and wild turkey every season of Tyndra's famine.

Many would die. Why not blame it all on the things that supposedly served the evil monster that lived, according to the old lore, near the forest's edge just inside the Ivy Wall: the swirling orange and blue barrier that separated heaven from hell and must always be feared and avoided as strongly as Odin must be worshiped and welcomed. *Ridiculous!*

A general mandate had been issued, just in case the old legend was true, by the border guards a few months back after a large pack of animals were spotted skulking and planning their next incorrigible plot. The guards, of course, assumed this recently missing baby had been stolen and most likely eaten in cosmic revenge and banned all pets, but no one had found any proof of the slaughter.

Footprints of a pack of wolves or wolf-like creaturesyes.

Little drops of blood that belonged to who knows what animal, here, and thereyes.

A mother's wails so loud they deafened her neighbors

before she took her own lifeyes. Three newly made orphans from that same devastated motheryes.

But no carcass.

No tattered clothes.

No lost doll.

And wasn't that a reason to be thankful instead of trembling with fear. *Not found.*

Talby slumped to the ground and begged. But there was no more food.

An insatiable void, a debt no amount of coins could ever satisfy, sunk to the bottom of Azza's stomach, and her abdominal muscles involuntarily clenched at the thought of their poverty. Instantly, the comforting heat from her core disappeared, consumed by the chill that swallowed everything that had ever existed in this gelid place she called home. And this Ivi shook and trembled with the chill of a life made of suffering in a world that seemed an awful lot like what Odin described as hell.

Surely she had enough food to feed a baby fox? What if she had children to raise? What did the others do? Maybe the children had starved, not gone missing?

She wondered briefly if the people of Tyndra had already died and served a sentence in Odin's hell of eternal punishment for some crime so ancient they had lost its memory.

Her chin fell to her chest, and her eyes dug into the floor looking for a reason to keep on living. *Ridiculous. Get over yourself, and get up.*

To stop herself from further depression, she quickly changed her perspective. She nuzzled the sweet, albeit innately selfish, little fox and promised to find a way to feed him more tomorrow, even if it meant she went without during the famine. Besides, she was an expert at going without. What was one more sacrifice to an expert in managing sacrifice like she?

Certain in the marrow of her bones there was some place better, some life worth living, some path worth forging, some seed she must plant or surely she would perish via the emptiness, she set her intention to make the best of her day and the sun's brief and dwindling light. Besides, she refused to buy into the malaise and apathy of frost heart that had already destroyed so many of Tyndra's weary villagers. These days, she had a fox to keep safe from the jowls of evil beastsboth the imagined and the real ones.

Azza threw her knees over the edge of the bed; they clamped down with moderate complaint. She pushed her fingertips down on her lower jaw to stop the chattering of her teeth and shook her head no while the tenderhearted, yet firmly spirited servant rose and stretched her long, muscular legs. It was earlywell before the brief appearance of the sun in Tyndra, yet she started her daily domestic duties anyway. She should have been angry to be up so early, hours before the other depressed villagers, but she didn't have tyme for such unpleasant feelings. Much like a fairy, her heart only had enough room for one emotionanger, fear, or gratitudeand this morning, she wanted to experience the good over the suffering. Besides, giving thanks kept her fear and loneliness far enough from her mind that it didn't take over her life. And above all else, Azza hated being afraid and alone.

So she thanked the cold, hard floor for keeping her from landing on the tundra below it. She bowed to the rotting beams above her head for finding the courage, much like her, to hold up the weight of its burden another day before collapsing. Azza pulled her arms in tight and clapped for the walls that, despite a few cracks, kept most of the roaring, icy wind from getting in. Taking out tomorrow morning's ration of stale bread, she gave half to the fox, and ate the rest herself. Thankful for the constant rumble in her tummy that demanded she get up each morning to find a way to feed it, she smiled at her adorable fox.

"Hunger is not such a bad thing, Talby," she said.

As if the fox heard the growl of his own belly and felt differently, he quickly disappeared into a crack in the wall Azza had, as of yet, been unable to discover.

She laughed and shook her shoulders to mimic the creature. Unable to resist it any longer, a simple song gathered in her throat and demanded she hum it out loud. She figured why bother hold it in. No one could hear her in the morning above the daily hailstorm anyway, so she rolled her full hips to the rhythm of her made-up song while she swept and tidied her small room, making her best attempt to also honor the few meager possessions she owned. Before long, the tune grew and grew until she realized she was singing at full volume, and she laughed again at the pleasure of hearing her own voice.

She paused in thought: not depressed was one thing, but being truly happy was a whole different thing. Happy was not allowed here in Tyndra and certainly not openly and for no reason other than because.

She dropped her shoulders, shifted her weight to the right, and looked at the ground searching for some misery to hold on to firmly. Quickly, she found it: the way her mother had suffered while giving birth to her and applied the mandatory flat mask of Tyndra. She held on to the image of her mother suffering long enough that her lips curved down to seal the pact of sadness. Even she knew it was an act though; at any moment she could snap out of her misery by simply humming the tune, offering up her gratitude for a few simple things. To prove it, she allowed herself just one morsel of gratitudeher song and the sweet company it offered her in her dreary and dilapidated home. And so she sang one more verse on the inside to shield her core from the pain she had to wear on the outside to fit in with the rest of her people.

She then recited her regular morning prayer for all those villagers who had already suffered enough to merit their death, thus, accomplishing a successful exit from a life of loss supposedly made to teach some elusive and ever-changing lesson she had never quite been able to decipher. *Why is the lesson always changing? How will I ever learn it?*

"Family and all those I have lost from this wretched and terrible life, may your souls finally find rest and peace in Ardnyt. May the warm sun feel delightful on your frozen and heavy shoulders and may, unlike here where we are broken and unworthy creatures, His abundance meet your every step in Ardnyt. May Odin bless you with the glory of His undeserved forgiveness in your final resting place."

It seemed to her she had been placed unwillingly in a game without being told the rules and then been punished for not being able to recognize the prize no one had shown her. She knew the prayer was supposed to give her hope, but for some reason, she hated saying it. As a child, she was told to welcome solace and know a higher power would grace her in a beautiful way after she had suffered enough to merit divine mercy, but somehow that never settled her deep inside. In fact, she considered that total absurdity, bordering on insulting.

Briefly, she questioned Odin's willone that took a child from their mother or a mother from their child...but then thought better of her blasphemy when she remembered how much worse things could get.

She quickly said the prayer again, remembering her place: small, little, unassuming. Besides, she had an okay life. Better than most even. Who the hell-of-Tyndra was she to question and doubt and ask for something more than what she already had? Asking for more was greedy, and she might be punished for that.

"Forgive me, Odin," she said, slumping her shoulders down and making her breath shallow and her body motionless. Her whispers sounded so low and foreign she wondered whose voice was coming out her pinched lips. *Surely not my own.*

She wanted to hum her song to soothe herself but suddenly couldn't recall its melody anymore. *Go, go, go. Work, work, work. Repeat. Do not ask for more than this life, you stupid child.*

Disgruntled and miserable, but done with her usual prep work and ready for the actual workday, she laid out her three ancient hand-me-down sweaters, their wool threads scratchy and surprisingly thin considering their purpose.

Purposeshe considered the meaning of the word: the reason for which something was done or created. Was her sweater's purpose to warm her or remind of her life of lack and loss? The prison door of Tyndra's ubiquitous poverty slammed her against the wall.

Surely everything had a purpose, right?

What is my purpose then? To suffer, of course.

As far as she was concerned, suffering was option. Painperhaps not. But the feeling of powerlessness to do anything about the pain that caused the sufferingyes. *Screw you, suffering. I am not poor even though I have no money.*

She looked at the picture of her beloved grandmother on her meager nightstand. *Not poor at all with a heart so full of love.*

She felt the wonder and joy inherent within her gather force again. But there was no time for such luxury. Hadn't the holey sweater done its job and reminded her? She had to go to work to earn tonight's meager food shares, so she banished the frivolity of her useless emotions and worried about fixing the sweaters instead of fixing a better life for herself and that fox.

Yet again, her thoughts briefly lingered on the word *purpose* and hung there like the frozen drops of water forming icicles on the limbs of the desolate old tree stump out front of her shanty quarters. Funny how those drops, abandoned by the clouds above, held on to something so dead, hoping to delay their inevitable *purpose* of joining and maintaining the penetratingly frozen landscape of her kingdom, aptly known as Tyndra.

"Purpose. Everything has a sad and wintry purpose or it is surely eliminated here, Azza," she remembered her Nana say during one of their conversations some ten years prior.

Azza, so young at the time, was obviously still convinced the unending ice of her reality would never freeze the center of her spirited character and turn her to stone like so many of the others she knew.

"The goal then, Azza, becomes living your purpose through grace before you die because you have missed it like a fool or turned to frost heart yourself. Then, unlike so many, you will be ready to see the lessons of Ardnyt are no different than the lessons of Tyndra once you get to the heart of the matter. These seem totally opposite but are actually exactly the same. Are you paying attention? Will you find the heart of the matter so you can find the way out? Or are you just another idiot imprisoned by the illusion, my child?"

Azza dug her index finger into her oldest sweater, confirming the location of the largest hole and sighed. *A holey sweater for a holey life.*

"Maybe I am an idiot, but maybe not. At least I am not holey," she replied as if her nana could respond. She sighed again, lighter this time, while she pulled her finger back and tried uselessly to make the tattered fabric whole again. *Some things are too damaged for fixing.*

She rubbed her sore right shoulder and carefully used her left arm to braid her pencil-straight, black hair into a tight rope that hung to her mid back. Considering how hard a braid can whip under a harsh gust of wind, she tucked the length of it under itself firmly and efficiently.

"So maybe, even though you left me all alone, I am getting smarter every day Nana," she announced, quite pleased with her cleverness. "And…if I wear the white tunic backwards, the holes won't line up with the gray one, and air won't get in. So, I don't even have to fix it, to fix it. If I can define the problem, I can find the answer. And if I can find the answer, then…" Chills shook her from head to toe as she replayed her words.

"Who's an idiot now? Surely not me," she said to her grandmother's picture on the nightstand while she clasped her metal vest into position and donned her gray leather boots.

Talby came back for one more trip around the room, and Azza quickly corrected herself after remembering the chills a few moments before. *What is the real problem here? Am I really alone? Have I ever been alone?*

"I am not alone. I have Talby, and I have you, Nana," she said, pulling her shoulders back up straight and certain.

The scratched and glassless silver picture frame beautifully surrounded the sweet eyes of her wrinkled face and protected it from the splinters of a makeshift table that should have been burned as firewood years ago. It and the picture it cradled with such affection was the one almost fine thing Azza owned, and she treasured it beyond measure.

"Drop that frame, fail your purpose, and I'll burn you. I swear it." She nodded her head with vigor at the table. Surely even a table as useless as it knew she meant that threat.

But Azza, unlike that pathetic excuse of a table, still didn't know her greater purposethe one deeper and more significant than turning the king's Irminsul three times to the right and three times to the left.

She imagined the prized objectthe Irminsul, a symbol of

Odin's promise to protect His people as given to them by one of the Norn sisters.

"Oh we need you now, Odin. Where are you? And why have you forsaken us? Do you not love your children?" she asked and dropped her eyes slightly.

The Irminsul, a thick staff standing at least six feet high, was made from the pure black tusk of some forgotten creature that had once roamed these lands before the ground froze and killed almost everything but the hardiest of people and animals. The top portion, measuring a foot or so across, was forged of flawless, impenetrable steel and shaped like the span of a fine bird's powerful wings. A delicate silver inscription had been carved by an unknown hand in a circular pattern down the length of the pole which ended in a metal cup that bore its way deep into the earth to hold the pole upright against gravity.

She pretended to spin the grand column, hoping Odin might hear her prayer more clearlythree full turns to the right, then the left. The effort, terrible yet invigorating, left both her right shoulder sore and her breast muscles firmer than the other women in her village, which she rather liked now that she thought about it.

After blowing her warm breath into her hands, Azza fastened on her reinforced gloves, pulled her ice goggles down low and tight across her brow, and stepped outside. At least she performed her duties for the king with pride. Never once had she been late or failed to turn the piece to the king's satisfaction. Next month would make five years, just two years shy of the longest anyone had survived her position.

She thought of her three sisters and smiled briefly before the wintery landscape froze that drop of pleasure, too. *The Irminsul will not get the best of me.*

As her feet carried her one way, away from the meager pleasures of her simple home and Talby, her mind swirled there still. Unconsciously, her grandmother's incantation flowed like music through her mind in preparation for the work always given only to the women of the Ivi clanthe clan that, after her, would be no more.

Twirl the Irminsul of Tyndra,
Which pierces truth with snow.
Locked by the vines of the Ivy Wall,
Two fates, each soul ought know.

Some time and miles later she arrived as usual trepidation filled her heart. *Can I hold the pole long enough? Twist it hard enough? Will my arm make it one more day? Why is this my purpose? And what will happen when there are no Ivi women left to perform it?*

Pulled from her thoughts, she heard the arrogant captain of the king's guards scream her name from the drawbridge, and so she ran to find out what the hell-of-Tyndra he wanted.

Chapter Two

LIKE CHALK ON A WRITING BOARD, the captain's voice sent shivers down her spine. Was he the one who had shot Talby's beautiful mother? Probably. *What an ass.*

Eyes fixed on the ground so they wouldn't betray her opinion of that creep, she walked quickly, but not too quickly, in response to his usually unreasonable demands. After all, Henrik had the authority to hang her on the spot. She wondered why he hadn't, especially since he was such a complete jerk so enraptured with his own power. Then she realized why: she was the last of her line.

Azza laughed under her breath, fogging up her ice goggles. Funny how her fragility was what gave her an advantage over that heartless jackass.

"You are late like always, Ivi, and I need to close these damn doors." He grunted and kicked a scrawny, black cat across the room. "Nasty vermin," he bellowed. His lip curled. "Both of you," he muttered under his breath.

She removed her glasses to see him better, now certain he had been the one who shot the defenseless fox. *You are the vermin.* He avoided her eyes.

Azza rounded her back and fanned her hands out in complaint at Henrik's treatment of another creature just trying to survive this life. After landing on all four paws, the cachectic feline hissed at the man. Azza nodded, dying to match the sound but unable to hiss like that.

She looked at the tymepiece above the painting of Tyndra's strikingly beautiful king and wondered why he had never married. Surely his good looks, flawless skin, high and regal forehead, and his once blonde, bouncy curls warranted the hand of a gorgeous bride at his side. Maybe he had always been a bachelor at heart, or maybe it was the empty chests in the treasury and the constant snow on the ground that kept potential queens away. Who, other than Odin, could possibly have said?

She nodded her head to the ticking of the clock and confirmed her own position on the matter. *Not late—two minutes to spare.*

"I have a mind to commit you to fifty lashes for such blasphemy of a servant in your purpose of service. Not here before the ringing of the bell. Petulant slave."

Purpose. I hate that word, she thought. *Yet I freaking hate you more, you arrogant prick. Colder than the Witch Saccas' tit that fed you curdled milk, you are.*

As if he saw the image of the withered breast of the beastliest witch of them all in Azza's mind, Henrik glared at her, his face made of hate so wide and distorted that it swallowed the world in cinnabar rage.

She matched his stare, measure for measure. *And I do hope you die from suckling it so long,* she added to the curse, wishing with all her will that she would have the courage to tell him how she really felt about him one day soon.

The massive clock struck its bell six times to mark the hour. Azza had been right—right on tyme.

Henrik flushed and looked away. "Must get that device

recalibrated to accurate tyme," he said as if somehow the hollow claim could save him from drowning in a river of his foolish assumptions.

Azza smiled. "Yes, that seems wise, my Captain. Or"she winked"you will never know who is on tyme and who is late. Then, oh my Odin, how will you ever know when to hang them?"

He quickly turned away.

While Azza tried to flatten her lifted cheeks, the captain bent over to adjust his boot. His collar shifted slightly to the side while he pretended to check the sole of his shoe and mumbled out a few profanities.

And that was when she saw his mark. *What!*

She gasped, her eyes as wide as the thick Ivy Wall that grew between the heaven-of-Ardnyt and hell-of-Tyndra whilst a thousand vines strangled her.

Oh my Odin, it simply cannot be!

The mark was cold and black, not fiery red, yet undeniably bore the same shape from her dreama diamond at the nape of this bastard's neck.

Chapter Three

UNABLE TO STOP HERSELF, Azza bounded forward in shock and accidently touched Henrik's shoulder. It was a punishable crime for sure, but suddenly she didn't care.

She had to touch it. She simply *must* despite a million layers of *shouldn't*.

Was the diamond mark cool or burning hot like in the dream?

She touched him again, not on accident, and sucked in her air.

"What the hell-of-Tyndra? Indignant slave!" He turned round, spit flying off the corners of his bared teeth. "How dare you touch meson of Hevius, captain of the honorable King Cassac!"

"Oh my Od…" she stammered, trying to roll her tongue back up into her mouth. She quickly thought better of the effort and let the second half of her God's name linger on her lower lip before she completed taking His name in vain and her muscular tongue back from her lower lip.

With a dying sun, in a dying world, the only orphan remnant

of the Ivi clan, what bit of life could this wretched man take from her that this wintry world had not already stolen?

She examined Henrik through the eyes of a fox: self-inflated warmonger with ominously dark brown hair cut short to his bullish head, chiseled face marked with two scars in the corners of his angry mouth. His height was slightly taller than average, his eyes sunken deep within their pits always scanning nervously to find another way out.

His chest, broad and wide, heaved with the fury of a bull determined to draw blood. But instead of cowering, she straightened her back and gracefully said, "Fine Sir, I forgive you for bumping into me. Twice."

His eyes sunk farther in.

"I must learn to step back more quickly. Forgive me now, please."

Farther in still.

Louder, she added, "Captain Helrick? Or is it Henrik? I can't ever seem to remember anything properly these days," and waved her skirt slightly to tease the animal inside him. She wiped her lip dry.

His eyes, unable to retreat farther in his head, popped out the other direction.

"Your grace," she said sarcastically, briefly forgetting all about the diamond on his neck.

He tried to shake the steam shooting out from his boiling eyeballs but failed.

Azza sighed and shrugged. "Your honorable king awaits my personal attention to his Irminsul. Shall I, then?"

Henrik's jaw smacked his heaving chest in awe.

She mumbled the mandatory chant.

"Twirl the Irminsul of Tyndra,

'Which divides truth with snow.

'Locked in the vines of the Ivy Wall,

'Two fates, each soul ought know."

The Captain Henrik, nostrils sputtering, was too shocked to speak. And in a haze of confusion, he allowed her to pass. She should have been imprisoned for such an intrusion on his sacred space, but by the tyme he remembered that, Azza had already reached the king's personal entrance.

The door slammed shut like the lid of a coffin, and the image of Azza's older sister, Elle, filled the captain's mind. He had loved her as much as his fickle heart had ever allowed him to love anythingsecretly from afar before she disappeared. He should have prevented it. Guilt chiseled at his cold and aching heart.

He replaced the emptiness and pain with rage and snarled.

In contrast, the joy in the king's voice drizzled out his chambers and lightened the entire castle. "Ah, Ivi, so good to see you this morn. We need you. Come here and spin my faltering Irminsul."

Henrik snarled at the momentary sliver of delight in the king's voice. This world was no place for delight, and he further squashed his memory of the possibility of an Ivi's joy quickly, spit on the slate floor, and dug into his suffering. The ache felt terrible, but at least he knew what to do with terrible. Besides, didn't the king know the faces of the Ivi sisters caused nothing but pain? Hadn't the king noticed the fine split down the middle of the Irminsul as if Odin himself had sent the message of what was to come? Tyme was almost at its end. The wolves were growing in numbers. The pruning was near. The legend was true. And didn't the king know that nothing but pain was real? Joy was an illusion, a promise only kept in Ardnyton the other unreachable side of this life, past the Ivy Wall. But most important of all, didn't he know by now the only way to get across that green wall and find promise of peaceful rest was in death, because no one made it through alive.

Chapter Four

KING CASSAC'S voice trembled slightly while he spoke. But oddly enough, the power of his broken and cracked words seemed unaffected by the fatigue inherent within them. As if perhaps, Azza noticed, the faults in his speech were an illusion and belonged to the person spoken to and not the royal mouth that spoke them.

Azza smiled, certain her king was an enigma she would never understand.

"Sing to me, Ivi's child," the ancient sovereign uttered while he grasped his canvas pillow like a child might have held a tattered bear and rocked back and forth. As he rocked gently down the river of memories in his mind, she lost him to another tyme, maybe all the way back to a better life in a better world.

Dementia. The tragedy of a mind lost in a maze of its own making.

"Yes, my King," she said to the beautiful elder and wondered what depth must exist under such a flawless face. Surely Odin had graced this man with an angel's complexion that seemed so perfect despite his obvious age and diseased mind.

But the watermarks of his journey dripped off of him and gathered force before filling the room with rapids swirling in lost possibility. The stench of his confused distraction infused the room, and the petals of his stolen innocence poisoned the rafters that held up the ceiling.

Instantly, the room grew so large it took Azza's breath way. She felt honored to have spent so many hours close to such a wise, benevolent leader even if he was nothing more than a child trapped in his own madness now. She imagined that in the heaven-of-Ardnyt, the monarch must look exactly like King Cassac on his throne.

"Dearest child, did you know that I remember back so long?" he asked, as he rolled his head side to side with the tenderest gaze in his eyes. "So long ago."

"Yes, please tell me," she replied, hoping he would tell her a story he had not told her before.

"Once this cold and barren world was very different."

"Before the dawn of tyme happened, you mean?"

"Yes. Before. You." He laughed like he might give away more information than he should.

Azza assumed her position next to the great staff and sat down eager-eyed to listen better. "Please tell me. My grandmother told me so many wonderful stories, and I loved them so."

The king's eyes cleared and focused on her. "Yes, dear, once the people of this world were free to choose from one side to the other. There were cold places and hot places and ways to move easily between them. Cloudy skies and clear skies. Ice and fire. And love… there was that, too. Love's first kiss."

"Oh do tell me a love story, please."

"Yes, but you must not tell anyone I have told you the biggest secret of all."

"Pinkie promise."

"Pinkie promise…then that is enough for me, dear child. The secret is that it was never just a story." The king winked.

Azza realized she didn't have him for long. He was already slipping back towards crazy. She sighed.

"Sweet Ivi, have you ever noticed the letters atop that Irminsul you twirl?"

She hummed. "Maybe. What do they mean?"

"Correctionwho do they mean?" The king laughed sarcastically. Azza briefly felt shamed by him, but then she remembered how fragile his mind was these days and replaced her shame with compassion.

"Okay then. Who do they mean? Go on."

"I did it, you know. Who am I kidding? She'll never figure it out."

She had lost her monarch for sure now.

"Let me explain…." He began, and she hoped, oh how she hoped, he would finish this story unlike so many before it. He told her a legend of the youngest of the four Norn sistersa fickle little immortal thing who was always falling in and out of love with this or that. Of how her vengeful heart got the best of her when Za trapped herself in a tomb and split *time* into *tyme*, as the people of Tyndra knew it now, from the pain of losing her older sister.

Azza's heart ached from the memory of her sisters at this point, and she leaned in to hear the rest of the story better even though she knew the king was drifting faster and faster in and out of dementia.

As he described Za's need to spread her suffering to countless others for so long, a gentle tear streamed down his face as if this were more than just a storyas if he had been witness to the pain.

"My Grace, but I thought there were only three Norns," Azza said.

"Of course you did. Now there are three. But once there were four."

"Terrible."

"You have no idea," he said, wiping the stray tear away. Suddenly, he smiled and said, "Oh good, Azza, you are here. I wondered if you would be on tyme today. I think something must have gotten in my eye. See, it is wet."

She wanted to ask about Za's revenge, about what had really happened, but she didn't dare suggest his memory had failed him so severely. And so she played along with his momentary confusion, like always, and acted as if she had just arrived.

Cassac, the old fool, recited his usual greeting to her for a second time, and she stared at the floor, trying not to feel sorry for him. He would have never wanted her to feel sorry for him, of that she was absolutely certain.

She focused on the beautiful pattern in the old wood floor, not the sweet and handsome face of the king. Such a lovely face it was, so smooth and false in its witness to his aged suffering. But soon the floor bored her, and she looked back at him with hopeful anticipation. He smiled again, obviously pleased by her attention in such a way that made her wonder what other secrets were lost in his imploding mind.

"I do love our visits, youngest of the four Ivi sisters."

"Me too. Thank you. Are you in pain at the loss of your memory, my Lord?" she asked, searching for some trivial thing to soothe him. If she had a soft blanket she would have offered it without hesitation.

"Now that is a funny question? Am I in pain? Why would you of all possible people ask me that?" He wiped his eyes once more.

She quickly recovered. "The eye. Yes, your eye. My Liege, are you in pain?"

Cassac cleared his throat. "Sing. I demand it."

"But?" the last living Ivi asked, squinting her left eye.

"Sing. There isn't much tyme left now. But you, dear, are becoming more aware of it, are you not? Don't answer that. Sing. Sing. Your king demands it."

And so she began her song again.

"Twirl the Irminsul of Tyndra,

Which divides truth with snow.

Locked in the vines of the Ivy Wall,

Two fates, each soul ought know."

Azza tried to stop, but Cassac was having none of it. "Go on. I do love that song. Oh how well it has served me," the king whispered before drifting off to sleep.

She sighed and continued, softer now.

"Swirl the Irminsul of Tyndra,

Which enslaves both friend and foe.

But one that came of the Ivy Wall,

Fates unite- or one must forever go."

The king mumbled something about sunlight and diamonds, which made no sense to Azza. Until she remembered her dream, that was.

Briefly, she allowed the dream and the boy with eyes of colors wrapped inside colors too gorgeous to name to consume her mind. A face she hated quickly replaced it instead. Henrik. *The diamond.*

The king startled awake. "Yes, maybe you do know more than you think you know, my dear." The king coughed. "As you spin, tell me a story now. My turn to listen." He winked.

Maybe he remembered more than he let on? But probably not. Who, other than Odin, could possibly say?

The king argued until she began the original version of Cinderella, the one before those brothers altered it.

When she finished, she added, "Not that it makes any sense

why a good father would choose such a terrible second wife…
but I guess fairytales rarely do. And why do all the good fathers
die? And all the bad fathers live? And why does the maiden
always run out of tyme?"

The king laughed so hard he almost fell over. "What would
you say," the king asked, "if I told you that you were made of
tyme? That you are tyme?"

"I would beg your pardon and suspect you really had lost
your mind?"

He clicked his tongue. "Is that what my people say about
me? Oh my."

Her cheeks flashed crimson, and she tapped her heels on the
lovely floor.

"Dames of the Ivi have never minced words. The truth
stains your face. And marches your feet."

With one final tap, Azza bowed respectfully and placed her
hand upon the Irminsul she had just rotated so skillfully.

"It is good"the King grinned"that you were the last frond to
grace us with your blossoming touch. Your skills are the best of
all who came before you, and the pruning would have already
happened years ago had you not been so excellent in your
working of the Irminsul's dance with the sisters of Norn."

"What?" Azza asked, now meeting the king's gaze and
trying to decipher if this last sentence was the riddle of a genius
or the blabbering nonsense of a fool.

"Never mind. Thanks be to Odin and his absence for
keeping us here so long. Do not worry your pretty little twigs of
hair."

"Thanks be to Odin," Azza replied, more confused than
before and almost sure the king really had lost his mind. *Twigs
of hair? Really?*

She fluffed the king's pillows and twirled the Irminsul for
one last measure as Cassac drifted off to sleep again. As she

backed away from it, she prayed to Odin that no more children would go missing this night.

As if it were Odin's denial to her prayer, a thunderous slam assaulted the roof of the castle. She should have trembled but refused. Unlike all the others in Tyndra, she had this odd idea that fear was some kind of illusion, a trick used against them, a ruse to trap them in this frozen place. Each time she swirled the Irminsul, her confidence in her theory grew as if her inner knowing got more powerful with each turn. But oddest of all, she sensed that the Irminsul, a gift left here by the hand of Odin Himself, directly contributed to that fear.

Something hidden deep insider her told her there was more than fear, more than pain, more than hunger and cold limbs outside the confines of her awareness. Something she must learn or remember or understand.

So instead of trembling, she went to find Henrik and get a better look at his mark. Much to her surprise, he was just on the other side of the door and almost fell down when she opened it.

Chapter Five

HENRIK CLEARED his throat and said, "Woman. Last of the Ivi, come with me." His eyes zigzagged like the guilty straps of a leather muzzle across a dog's snout.

What a jerk. Look at me!

He sucked in his breath and held on to the air. "El..." he stammered.

"Elle is gone. Azza. My name is Azza," she said, confused that he, of all people, couldn't even remember her name. Of course, she had no idea about his unrequited affection for Elle, her dead and gone sister who could have been her twin.

"Az... Azz... Azza." He laughed, unable to finish his sentence.

"Yes?"

He slapped his hand on his thigh although Azza had no idea why. "Your sister, I..."

"Is dead. Yes, they are all dead. Your point, Captain, is..."

He looked at the floor. "I am sorry. You were on tyme earlier. My error, I am afraid," he said as if he actually had feelings other than hate and rage.

Azza stood her ground and plastered another layer of indifference across her face. *Not possibleHenrik a human? You're famous for a brow of steel, a cruel heart, and no mercy, no apologies.*

Perhaps there was more to him than met the eyes. But probably not.

They were startled by the first of many screams and the gunshots that followed in the distance, and she knew another child had gone missing.

Chapter Six

"ANOTHER CHILD!" Henrik hollered and scrambled for his ice ax and rifle. But before he could locate the proper equipment, another guard ran into the castle and confirmed their worst suspicions.

Blood stained the guard's tattered uniform.

Henrik gasped. "Where? Where, soldier?"

"One thousand meters from the Ivy Wall. Five red wolves and a toddler. Martha's only child. The one with the shriveled hand. First her husband to frost heart from the pain of having the deformed child. Now the child's gone, too."

"Tell me you tried to save it!" Henrik screamed.

"We failed you, Captain."

"You failed the child, not him, you ass," Azza accused.

"She will surely kill herself next. Poor Martha," Henrik said and pointed at the terrible red stains.

Azza whimpered. "The poor child."

"We fought hard, but the wolves fought harder. They were so strong, like magic possessed them with its power," the soldier added, unable to stand still and shifting his weight from one side to the other.

"So much blood for a baby," Azza mumbled.

"No. Not the baby. You don't...not the baby. Jordidiah's legpierced by the fangs of the largest of the five wolves."

"Five! Why so many?" Henrik asked as if anyone had the answer to his question.

"Jordi... he tried to hold on to that baby. Almost saved it, but the largest wolf, the one with the biggest talons would have killed them both," the soldier claimed.

"Show me. Show me, now!" Henrik saluted the man.

"Are you telling me," Azza said, "that the legend of the wolves living in the Ivy Wall is more than just an old story?"

Henrik snorted. "So much more terrible than wolves. Mutant wolves with wings and talons, and if you listen at just the right tyme, the roar of a lion."

Chapter Seven

HENRIK IN THE LEAD, he and his soldiers advanced north through the open snow towards the Wall of spiraling Ivy leaves that separated the hell-of-Tyndra from the heaven-of-Ardnyt before they were forced to take cover about two hundred meters from the thick layers of glass in between two worlds. The scaffolds of jagged rocks blocked at least some of the terrible winds that whipped their chapped and pinched faces as they approached the divide between the two existences that couldn't have been more different.

Each passing moment, the storm seemed infinitely worse than the last, and even the most optimistic observer would have realized the futility of their plantrudging through mounting ice and snow to find a toddler stolen by animals that were likely already hiding in the most discrete of lairs. Even if they found the wolves' hiding place, how would they battle with inadequate numbers of men and scant supplies against the pack of mutant creatures?

"Stay behind that boulder, woman," Henrik demanded. "You will endanger the mission."

She placed the muzzle of his gun to her chest and coughed.

"Then shoot me, and I won't be able to walk beside you while I patch up my wounds."

He grinned but quickly wiped it off of his face. "Fool," he said. "To the back then. I can't waste men saving you, too."

Azza stayed at the far back of the group at first, but she couldn't tolerate their stories about the women in the village and what went on behind dark curtains in the middle of the coldest storms.

She inched forward, sure now that Henrik was the least disgusting of the men. And the markhe wore the mark. She wanted to touch it.

Azza was stronger than most women and some of these men who were constantly concerned about the stick of flesh between their legs.

"I could take out every one of them," she warned the captain.

He nodded, fully aware of the fact she had won her fair share of arm wresting matches against men at the local pub.

Azza gripped the bo staff in her hand and gritted her teeth down hard against the ice forming on her upper lip. She would fight for the children if necessary, of that she was certain. "Probably you, too," she added.

"You're not kidding. Ha!"

"Nope."

Henrik recognized determination when he saw it and laughed. Maybe they were not so different after all.

Behind her, the strongest of the soldiers breathed heavily, trying to extract enough oxygen from the thin air to maintain consciousness. Not her. Not Henrik. Eventually, one by one, the men fell back or dropped to the ground demanding they retreat. Even an idiot could see this was going nowhere at all.

"Just a bit farther," Azza pleaded. "We must come close

enough to see the Ivy Wall. Do you think the fronds will freeze in this terrible storm?"

"Storm. You could call it that," he shouted, but she barely heard him over the wind. She thought he said something about pruning, too.

They were almost close enough to see the wall now. Azza had never been this close. Sure she had seen drawings and photographs but never the actual magical structure in person like this. It was simply forbidden to be so near the place where souls crossed over from the hell-of-Tyndra to the heaven-of-Ardnyt.

It was hauntingly beautiful with complexity beyond her ability to assimilate such a massive structure into a definition that would fit in her overwhelmed mind.

From Tyndra's side of the wall, loops of green Ivy with blue leaves swirled in a counter clockwise direction infused with inter-woven golden ropes of ethereal material so majestic she couldn't hope to describe it. Thick and strong and eerily powerful, it looked like someone had taken an eternity weaving the fine substance in just the right position to lock the ivy inside itself. Even more mysterious were the golden-red leaves that sprouted from the other side of the wall through its draping and swirling loops of ivy.

Even though she knew it was infinitely impossible to see where one color or one strand ended and another began, she tried to will them apart with focused intention so she could see them better.

"Insane, isn't it?" Henrik asked.

"Yes, I never…"

"I know. No one ever does."

She looked. She looked harder. She tried to unwind just one segment of one strand in her mind. "Oh my Odin." She covered her mouth and fell backward in shock.

"What? What do you see?" Henrik demanded.

The wolves' deafening howls echoed off the walls, and she screamed the scream of certain death. "A hand…in the wall. A baby's shriveled hand."

"The Enfield's curse!" one of the soldiers yelled.

Chapter Eight

IN TYNDRA, at the castle

A blank mask of strength shielded Henrik's face, but fear stained his eyes which glanced nervously around the room like a caged animal trying to find a way, any way out of its pen.

"You okay?' she asked.

"Okay? No. But at least we are alone. For a few moments anyway. Before the masses come running to gather the weapons to break down the wall. If they attack the Ivy Wall"–he pointed to the roof, which still echoed from the assault of hail, but his eyes went out of focus–"it will attack them back."

She was confused now. Did this cat kicker of an asshole really give a flip about the masses? The baby's handsure. Who wouldn't have dropped to their knees? But the masses...

"I've seen arrows, bullets, even fire come from..." He looked down. "No, I mean come through the wall. It's not just heaven's gate. There is something terrible living in that wall. Something magical. Something cursed. The pruning has begun."

"Cursed? But it's an old legend." Then she remembered what the king had said about the secret, about it being true.

"Many will die if we attack the wall. Not just the children. Maybe all of us." Henrik backed up, giving her room to move, but she couldn't.

She froze. *All of us, dead.* The heaviness in the room swallowed her, and her feet sunk like they were trapped in a pit of sand in the floor. Speechless, but still sinking into the quicksand of the thought, she stood there like a mute idiot looking for the right words that never came. She considered struggling so the sand would take her down faster. The waiting was the worst part.

He held his breath, sinking in the pit of misery with her. Finally, Henrik's need for oxygen got the better of him. He took another precious mouthful of air and shook his head in defeat at needing something so complicated as air amongst so much dirt.

"The pruning?" Azza asked. The king said that word earlier.

"It is in the legend, the name of the final battle of the war against tyme."

She found something to say and dug into it. "War? You mean the sun's ice storm as it slowly changes, right?"

He mumbled something she couldn't quite understand.

"Right?"

"Foolish Azza, child from the Ivi. I had hoped you weren't as stupid as the others. For Odin's sake, you, of all of these peons, spin the Irminsul. You hold the magic in your hands every day. What do you think keeps the wall in place? The Irminsul. Didn't you know what you were doing by turning it?"

"What the hell-of-Tyndra are you saying?"

"Didn't you know that was your purpose? To maintain the wall. It is the birthright of the Ivi. Your nameIvi."

There she went, sinking again.

"Surely you have noticed your own name? That only your family is allowed to touch the thing. That since you are the last…" He rolled his eyes and angrily squashed a spider on the floor, which seemed solid all of a sudden.

Azza decided that maybe she had given him too much credit earlier. The poor arachnid just wanted to live. Even ugly things had the right to survive.

He added, "The king, poor old man, seems to think you have some great potential. Once while half asleep, he even told me it was your destiny to decipher the riddle of the Za and save or kill us all. That I would help you do it. If only I… But that's ridiculous. Demented, that man, obviously."

Henrik blew the snot from his nostrils and wiped it away with his sleeve.

Now Azza was certain she had given him too much credit earlier. *Purpose? That word again.* "Excuse me, Helrik. Did you just call me a stupid peon?"

He shook his head and rolled his eyes. "Henrik. My name is Henrik. How many times do I"

"I am no child." She furrowed her brow and shook her finger at him. "Besides, I think we both know that I know your name, Henrik."

The fury slathered across Azza's face momentarily disguised the sweet innocence in her doe eyes, and Henrik decided that she, this spirited little thing, was way more beautiful than her sister had ever been. He wanted to kiss Azza, like kissing her would somehow fix everythinglove's first kiss, ah. But just because one legend, the Ivy Wall, was true, didn't mean anything about the rest of the fairytales. The power of love's first kiss was bullshit. His eyes quickly lost focus when he remembered that beasts were real, the magic of love was a lie.

"A big fat lie," he whispered.

Azza slammed her foot down to check the solidity of the floor.

He laughed, still floating in the thought of kissing her. Maybe just one kiss was worth the effort? Just to test his theory, to prove it wouldn't work. He tried to stop himself at the thought, but he couldn't. The flavor of this interaction felt so much better than the permanent loss of that baby that he suckled it up and tasted every delightful drop, savoring Azza's fury and loving it.

She stomped the floor once more, and he lost himself entirely to his desire.

Oh kiss me, Azza. Screw the legend, just kiss me. "Say it again. My name. Please, I'm begging you."

"Oh, you!"

"Helrik. That's funny. You are a clever string of Ivi, Azza. And beautiful. You are certainly that as well."

Was he messing with her now? She scowled.

"I mean that. No bullshit. Beautiful."

Azza grunted and turned away. The fullness of her backside did nothing but feed his desire to know more about her than he had ever known about anyone, including himself. There was something unique, above and beyond the perfection of her rear end, about this young Ivi the king held so dear, after all. Almost as if the entire world existed because of her, and she was the source of tyme. *Kiss me Azza Ivi. Again and again.*

Too bad they were all going to die before he had the chance to put the idea to the test and, even better yet, wrestle a few hot nights between the sheets out of her. He imagined pulling back her long, sleek, black hair while he placed his mouth over hers to get a better taste of her youthful flavor. What did she taste like? Probably like cinnamon mixed with cloves.

Warmth pulsed below his belt. He didn't have time for exotic thoughts like that though, so he shook the delicious spice from his mind and rolled his shoulders to prove he was able to shake it loose before she turned back around.

Just in case, he coughed and imagined an ugly old witch in Azza's place. Thankfully, the pressure in his center lessened enough for him to think.

He laughed, sarcastically this time, and resumed his razor sharp focus while she met his eyes once more. "Follow me or die sooner rather than later. The wolves are coming. The ice is coming. We are all as good as dead. The only question is how much tyme we have left."

"I refuse to believe that. There is always a way out." She thought about Za and briefly wondered if she had ever gotten out of her tomb. *How, Za? Show me how.*

"Who am I kidding? I think we both know I don't actually care about anyone but myself. Well maybe my men, too."

That pissed her off past the point of no return because she was sure it was true.

The banging on the roof reoriented her, filling her flushed ears with undeniable evidence of a problem far more serious than her superficially wounded pride. Her heart pounded, and her gut clenched. *Talby!*

The ice outside was harder and more terrible by the minute.

Talby? Are you ok? Had the wolves found him or the villagers shot him? The poor darling must be terrified. *Poor fox, so alone and scared.*

She shivered. Would the roof hold? *My sweet baby fox. I must save you.*

Henrik turned round to examine the faltering integrity of the weakened roof, and she remembered the mark. *Must touch the mark. Baby fox. Markhot. Poor Talby. Fire. Ice. Alone. Not alone.* Her thoughts flashed quicker and quicker.

"The roof won't hold much longer. Come quickly, Ivi, or go meet Odin at the pearly gates of Ardnyt," he said.

Startled by the undeniable need to touch that mark on his neck and hold on for a different lifeone with new possibilities, new discoveries, and new truthsshe grabbed his hand and held on tightly. *Markhot. Touch. Hold. Kiss. My hand in your hand. Hold me.*

A familiar scent rushed through her: musk, cinnamon, some exotic spice she knew no taste of or name forlike argon oil, only stronger and finer. The fragrance infused her with the certainty that she knew this man, knew the inside of this man, and that in some way, she had experienced this before.

His scent drew out her scent. Or did it draw hers in? More than adding, their aromas would multiply. Of that, she also felt certain.

Her mixed emotions surprised her: fear, excitement, and undeniable desire to understand him better, all at once.

Not sure who seemed more surprised, him or her, she came up tightly behind him and wrapped both her arms round his waist and sucked in a larger breath of that intoxicating scent while getting a better look at his neck. This was probably her last chance to touch another human being. She felt his buttocks rock forward and flex while he, too, obviously relished the sensation for a moment. *He likes me afraid and weak like this.*

But what he really wanted was lost to her.

She sighed, lost in her swirling thoughts. *The mark. What does it mean? What do you mean?* Was an answer hidden in it somehow? A secret worth uncovering? A truth that if not uncovered meant the loss of everything good?

Henrik felt her urge to uncover the truth in him and seriously considered spinning round to take Azza right then and there. He imagined grabbing her hard from behind against the trembling walls despite the cold drafts of air just like he had done, he suddenly remembered, more than once in his dreams of golden fields and flowing streams.

A thousand partial memories resurfaced, and he fell backwards form the pull of ither face, her hair, her scent, her juicy core.

He had loved Elle thinking she was the one in his dreams, but all these months, it had been Azza. Azza was the one he held and soothed through the night in a dream world almost unreachable from here.

Or was it? Was the dream Ardnyt? Did he dare hope that after death she would be the one waiting for him at heaven's gates? If so, he vowed to die right here and now for the promise of something more than all this suffering, and that gave him incredible strength.

He took a deep breath and decided to tell Azza his secret: the dreams, her sister, the mark on his neck, the mark that matched the one on Azza's chest that he had seen so often in his dream.

He gathered his courage, now more afraid of her rejection or dismissal than the ice and all the wolves that had ever howled. "I have to tell you something. I have to tell you now before the roof falls and I never get the chance to tell you."

"Yes?"

"In my dreams. You…"

Suddenly, the center of the roof lost its battle with the storm and fell in defeat.

She ran backwards, and he ran the other way. Now a pile of slate, once the proud roof of their castle, stood between them like the unspoken words. He must tell her. He simply must.

She wanted to climb across to reach him, to feel his strong muscles again. She needed him, needed to touch his mark once more before she died. The same as the mark on her chest. Yet something deep within told her he needed her more than she needed him. The thought felt delicious and dripped like honey she had never tasted from her full and pulsing lips.

But there was someone who needed her more: Talby.

Her thoughts flashed back and forth again. *Talby. Mark. Want. Wet. Pressure. Help.*

It was now or never; she had to decide which way to go. This man had the power to help himself. Talby didn't.

She chose the fox.

"I'm sorry," she screamed and ran the other way. She tried to explain, but Henrik didn't know about the fox. No one did.

He misunderstood and only saw her leave him. Just like they always did. No matter how strongly he fought or how many battles he won, they always left.

He would never be good enough. Never.

"I knew you could never want me. No one ever does," he said as he watched the woman of his dreams disappear to the other side of what had once been possible. And he knew, most likely, straight to her death.

The king had been wrong.

The chance to fix this, to stop the pruning, to save the children if they could…if there had ever even been one, was gone-just like his loveforever.

Chapter Nine

FROZEN, but still clinging to life, Azza made it the thousand meters due south to her quarters. The tree out front had fallen from the weight of the ice and snow, now so thick it went as high as Azza's knees with each step.

Once through the door, she dropped the bo and took off her ice goggles. If she were going to save that fox, she must have intense focus: fast, effective, driven, absolute certainty, no fear, only gratitude. These were the only things that could serve her to help save Talby. Although, what to do when she found him was her biggest problem, one she would have to deal with eventually if this went well: the guards would shoot Talby on the spot.

She scanned the room for a promise or an answer that just wasn't there to find. Nothing. More nothing. More. Her bed broken, turned on its right side. The small table, now in pieces, had failed its purpose after all.

"Talby!"

She swiftly leaned down to pick up the picture frame now broken in two pieces, removed the photo, and shoved it down her sweater. *Now, fox, where are you?*

The wall of her hut shifted, and the roof cracked. She didn't have long now.

The wind howled to warn her. Fear grabbed hold, and she called out to the creature again, louder this time. "Talby, Talby!"

Her worries scattered and pinged off the floor gathering speed. Where was Talby? Had the guards already found him? Was he already dead?

Her thoughts whirled faster. *Dying. Fox. Guards. Dead. Henrik. Talby. Poor baby fox.*

Even faster. *Babies trapped. Ivy Wall. Save them. Shriveled hand. Henrik, help me. Save me. Fox. Help. Dead.*

Thoughts too fast to contain. *Why didn't I stay with you? So stupid. Such a mistake.*

Deadly thoughts, swirling just like the storm outside. *Idiot, like Za. Trapped myself, like Za. Henrik! I am so stupid. I could be safe in his arms. Those arms. The mark. Diamond. Hot.*

Until now, she had fooled herself into thinking she had blocked out wanting Henrik, wanting to stay with him, the smell of him, the fiery red mark, the kindness he hid under his furrowed brow and tough exterior.

The roof shifted, and the crack spread down the north-facing wall, bringing her attention back. Without focus, she was as good as dead.

"Talby!" Her frantic scream was muffled by the crash of the roof caving in. She looked up through the open ceiling into the angry sky to see a huge ice ball careening straight for her head."

Three feet across, the monstrous hail mesmerized and simultaneously paralyzed her with its shiny white brilliance as it made its way towards her skull.

As if she were a deer caught in the light's trance, she couldn't move and just watched the deadly hail come to take her life. Many thoughts flittered through her mind as tyme stood still to allow this final moment of reflection.

Oddly enough, none of them were about her escape.

Talby, where are you? Are you safe? Are the children dead or just trapped like Za? What does dying feel like? Will anyone find and bury my body? Sisters, will you wait for me at the gates of Ardnyt after I have crossed the Ivy Wall to reach Odin's land of grace and abundance.

She felt Odin's hand touch her cheek and call her name. Maybe she was already dead, the ice ball already through the middle of her skull. How kind of her body to spare her so much pain in that terminal moment.

Dead wasn't so bad.

She would have reached up to feel her split head, but why bother?

She blinked her eyes softly in surrender to the sound of her name.

"Azza."

Her name Ivi, same as ivy only with one letter different, an "I" for a "Y". Does a letter really matter that much?

"Azza."

There it was, her name again. *Az plus Za.*

Funny how for the first time ever she realized her name was made of *Za,* both backward and then forward, to make the longer name Azza. Had someone named her that on purpose? Her dead mother perhaps?

Certain her body was nothing more than food for the wolves now, she blinked once more, hoping Odin would call her name a third tyme. *Azza.*

Or was it Za? Had it always been Za?

There was such a pleasurable intensity in the way Odin spoke Azza's name. Or was it Nido, Odin spelled backwards? She wasn't sure anymore.

Was there a difference in forwards and backwards? Maybe not. No, probably not. Azza remembered her grandmother's words about how things that are backwards and upside down are sometimes exactly the same.

"Azza," the voice said, strong this time, like a mature hart that claimed his mate amongst the coy members of his herd.

She smiled, but only with her eyes, knowing it must have been Odin who called her out.

"Move you foolish girl! Move!" the deep voice said.

She sighed deeply, her doe eyes sweet and soft, and dug into the light coming from above her splintered head.

A muscular and mighty arm wrapped tightly round her waist as Henrik pulled her from danger just as the ice ball landed where she had stood a split second before.

Breathless, she finally said, "Oh my, Odin."

The king's captain laughed again and said, "No, Henrik. Or is it Helrik? Now I can't seem to remember, either."

She coughed, brought back from the beautiful possibility of her own death, and tried to roll her eyes still inside her absolutely fine and intact skull. But much to her surprise, the words, "Thank you," escaped her mouth before she found a way to suck it back in.

"You're welcome," he said sincerely.

"But why did you come to find me?"

"Because I knew I must."

"You mean you should…"

"No, I must."

As if he agreed with Henrik's *must*, a small fox stepped out from the rubble and ran up to Azza to greet her like and old friend.

Chapter Ten

"YOU KNOW ABOUT MY MARK, I take it," Henrik said, scratching his neck. His fingers paused over his mark. The diamond now warm and seemingly getting hotter.

She smiled, still thinking about the fairytale of Za and the puzzle of her name.

"This is why you came back? A fox?"

"Yes. And the picture of my grandmother."

He groaned.

"What is it called when a word is the same spelled both right-to-left and left-to-right?" she asked and furrowed her brow deep in thought. She stepped forward and touched his mark, allowing her fingers to stay on top of his for a brief but delightfully sweet moment.

"What?" He shook his head, sure she had lost her mind, and sure that if she kept it up, he would lose it, too. "We must leave. The storm."

"Not without the fox."

"Idiot," his mouth said. His eyes said something quite different. "Grab the vermin. Shove him in your sweater. Pretend he's a cat or something. I will find a way to protect him. But know it's against my better judgment. How can that thing possibly help us, not hurt us?" Even though he squinted his eye in anger, his pleasure shined through the furious façade.

"Thank you," she said. Not even trying to hide her pleasure, she touched his face softly. She giggled, and he was ruined forever. His heart, too big now, would never fit back in his chest again.

Even though the words were obvious lies by this point, she said them anyway. "I still hate you, Henrik. Even more for saving me, but I like you more than I hate you now, and that is quite a twist of fate, don't you think?" She touched his face once more.

"A palindrome."

"What?"

"Words, the same forwards and back."

"Yes. Just like… Oh my…" Her jaw dropped and smacked her chest while the significance set in.

"What?"

"Azza. Ivi. And Cassac, just like that, too."

"King Cassac!" Henrik hollered, suddenly remembering he was supposed to be protecting the king. "Come fast, Ivi. We have wasted too much tyme."

"Yes. Wasted too much tyme. That's exactly what I've done. All these years," she said, taking his hand. They ran against the raging snow, both for different reasons: Henrik to do his duty and protect the king, and Azza to try to undo what she had done with a terrible spell so long ago.

Chapter Eleven

DESPITE THE WORSENING STORM, they made it back to the castle. Talby barked to prove he was on board for what was yet to come. Palpable relief washed over them once they reached the drawbridge, and Henrik risked embracing Azza. This tyme, she leaned in and welcomed it.

But screams broke up the delightful union prematurely. It was already too late. People scattered everywhere, running aimlessly like fools in terror.

"The king?" Henrik asked of another guard who looked as lost and afraid as a child unable to find his mother in a crowd.

He shook his head.

"No." Henrik said, already running.

The King was gonea piece of fur from his nightgown torn and splattered with blood suggested the unthinkable. The mutant creatures had taken him, just like all the precious children. The Irminsul of Tyndrapriceless offering of Odinhad split in two. One piece had landed in the corner of the large, barren room. The other piece was nowhere to be found.

Henrik, chest heaving, ran to the remaining piece. "Cassac,

you fool! I warned you that bitch was planning to attack us and split the Irminsul!"

He dropped his head in his hands, and his voice quivered. Azza couldn't be certain, but she thought she heard him say, "We are all dead now. The war against tyme has begun."

In the center of what had once been the king's bedchamber, a swirling cloud appeared and replaced the floor. Azza used to think the slate floor looked old, dingy, too cheap for the kind king's castle, even if Tyndra was an impoverish kingdom. All of a sudden, by comparison, it seemed the richest and grandest floor she had ever stood upon. Where was it now? Why couldn't she just wish it back?

The black funnel emitted a high-pitched, eerily penetrating sound that seemed to be the combination of innumerable voices screaming in paina cloud made of pure hatred and evil and suffering.

Azza wondered if this was what people meant when they used the phrase "hell-of-Tyndra", but before she had time to complete the thought, the pressure of the terrible sound pulled her towards it. She leaned forward and almost fell in, like somehow she belonged to the pit, like it belonged to her.

Henrik quickly grabbed her hand just before she disappeared into the abyss of eternal suffering, and they both knew they would be swallowed up in its spell if they didn't leave immediately.

"Run, Azza. Run. Run!"

For once, she did what she was told without hesitating.

As they ran, the walls of the castle tumbled down around them. Nearly missing Henrik's head, several beams crashed to the floor and were sucked into the collapsing center of all that used to make this place royal and fine.

"There will be nothing left soon. It is decided, " he told her and collapsed to the ground not ten feet outside the castle's frozen moat.

In the distance, the incessant howling began. Chills coursed down their spines in warning. The mutant wolves had come to claim the Enfield's final prize: the end of tyme in Tyndra.

Section II: In Ardnyt, on the other side of tyme

Are we not drawn onward, drawn onward to new era?

Madam, I'm Adam.
    Now Eve, we're here, we've won,
    Live on, Time; emit no evil.

Rise, sir lapdog! Revolt, lover! God, pal, rise, sir!
    "Revolt, love!" raved Eva. "Revolt, lover!"

No word, no bond, row on.

Live not on evil deed, live not on evil
    Eve damned Eden, mad Eve.
    Red Roses run no risk, sir, on nurses' order.

Draw, O Caesar, erase a coward.
    Never a foot too far, even,
    Sore was I ere I saw Eros.

Are we not drawn onward, drawn onward to new era?

- The Irminsul of Ardnyt

Chapter Twelve

In Ardnyt

Bored by the thought of even getting out of bed this morning, the nineteen-year-old princess groaned. The youngest, least informed, and surely the least important royal slave-to-the-people of Ardnyt yawned, desperately trying to drag back onto her a moment more of her intriguing and wonderfully reoccurring dream. The color of her hair in the slippery vision seemed indescribably more intense and more interesting to her than the shade of the night's sky at its darkest moment on its clearest night.

Deliciously simple, let me savor it longer. Please, I beg thee. Dear Nido, answer my prayer and trap me in my dream forever.

The young boy's eyes in the visiona rich and indefinable haze with colors within and underneath, colors so dark and enticing she had no name for but imagined, was certain even, must exist somewhere on the other side of the sky's crisp blue expanse. But just like every morning before this one, his eyes slipped perilously away before the minty breath of her chilled air had escaped her full and dripping lips.

Hungrily, she reached up to stroke the boy's neck and to feel the delightful chill of the inviting mark that defined him even more than those ebony eyes: a sable diamond-shaped scar, icy and more determined than the last flake of a legendary snowstorm of the old days to freeze eternally, just beneath the nape of his muscular neck. But painfully, the once frigid image was already ablaze like scalded milk that has curdled in a stainless steel pan, wasted, only to be eternally replaced by another jug of milk forever prepared to pour itself next into the pan.

Toby, an endearingly submissive baby wolf, obviously the beaten and abused runt of his litter, scurried across the room to greet the princess. Unable to resist the pleasure she found in him, she smiled despite her sadness from the stolen dream.

Briefly, she tried to bring the image back for one more refreshingly simple moment of joy, but to no avail. Thus, she offered her attention to the timid creature instead. The adorable blue-black wolf cried out, brave enough for once to demand the princess pet it.

"Well, I guess we are more alike than different, Toby. So many brothers and sisters that we shall have to love and amuse ourselves before we die from yawning." She laughed, and the small animal wagged his fluffy tail.

They yawned together as if to seal the pact between them.

One month prior, she had adopted the poor creature, amongst all the litters of pets, still trying to grasp his mother's attention. She adopted him before she had been assigned a pet by the guards. No one wanted the blue fox, so she did.

Blue-black, the color so intense and gorgeous, was a rarity in this kingdom. And the myth of the blue fox bringing bad luck in the form of deadly misfortune was nothing more than a fairytale written by the Brothers Grimm. The princess, unlike most of the villagers, had read the stories that her people took to be truth. Fairytales are turned by fear into vehicles to grow more fear. Fear, the fuel for more fear, a terrible and vicious cycle only cured with so much gratitude there was no room left for the fear.

The people who randomly passed out the wolves were idiots, and the only thing worse than an idiot was a careless idiot just doing what he was told for the sake of doing it. Wolves, like children, should be chosen, not doled out.

Toby growled; clearly he agreed with the princess's thought process. Or maybe he was just saying he was thankful she had picked him amongst so many other choices.

"I'm sorry, Toby. Everyone needs to be special. Even me. I'll be your special friend by choice, not decree, and you can be mine. Deal?"

Pets were now mandatory for the general population. Mandatorylike her fine clothes, the multiple layers of undergarments despite the terrible heat, the make-up sliding down her face, and the jewels strangling her neck.

A profound saturation, a surplus no amount of leeching could ever relieve, bloated her stomach, and her abdominal muscles involuntarily clenched. Instantly, the comforting coolness from her core disappeared, filled up by the overflowing heat and clutter that ruined everything that had ever existed in this scorching place she called home. If only she could put it all in a secret closet and lock it forever.

The Ivy Wall popped into her mind. *Locked forever, like monsters.*

But this sweet little child refused to wither away from a life made of gluttony in a world that seemed to her an awful lot like hell instead of heaven. She wondered briefly if she had already died and served a sentence of eternal punishment like Za for some crime so ancient she had lost the memory of it. *Ridiculous. Get over yourself, and get up. Better yet, get out.*

"If I was the one locked in that tomb, Toby, I would have

surely found my way out by now. Don't you think?" She nuzzled the small creature and promised to find a way to give it enough adventure, enough specialness. She once heard of a great wolf that had literally died of boredom. Toby would not die that way, she would make sure of it.

Certain in the marrow of her bones there was some better way, some life worth living, some clear and simple path worth forging, some seed she must plant or surely she would perish via the gloating, the malaise, and apathy of burn soul that had already destroyed so many of Ardnyt's blasé villagers. So she set her intention to make the best of her day and the sun's long and expanding light. Besides, she had a wolf to keep strong from his boring life where nothing mattered, where nothing was unique or interesting, and no one ever did anything challenging.

She threw her bare, flawless knees over the edge of her fine and highly vaulted bed. The joints clicked with complaint in anticipation of the two-meter drop to the padded mat waiting on the floor. A warning, she suspected, offered up by her frail bones before the slam of her petite and delicate feet down to the ground. Sometimes she wondered if she would shatter right there and end it all one morninga perfect splintering to excite her spiritless morning just as she finally died. Maybe that would get somebody excited about something.

She jumped down, despite the inherent danger, and groaned with the effort. She briefly considered doing it again for fun. But why bother? What would she gain other than thicker, stronger muscles? Was there any other choice, another way, something so different she hardly had the power to imagine such an existence? One that would spare her tiny feet such a burden to carry her weight another day?

"Leave me to my dreams in lieu of all this wondering, Nido," she sarcastically begged. If she thought it would have changed things, she would have dropped to her knees in prayer.

But the Goddess Nido had never granted her wishes, never even answered her questions. Why should this one have been any different?

I'd give it all upmy royal status, all these fine and dreadful thingsfor another moment of cold bliss with that boy in my dreams.

Like a message of hot denial, the room flushed with warmth, and she decided not to bother bargaining any further. Surely there was no point.

She fanned her neck to slow the dripping sweat, stood up straight, and arched her back, playing her daily game of trying to find something worth focusing on. She looked round the chamber, which an outsider might have described as glorious and grand, and aimed to remember the purpose of some of the infinite possessions she owned before her maids arrived to dress her.

Ah, the maids. So many damn servants, yet I am the real slave!

It could have been worse. She could have been stuck with one of her ridiculous, but undeniably perfect sisters determined to scorn and tease her for her immaturity and innocence. If only she had been the sole surviving princess in her family, perhaps this life would have seemed more livable to her. But alas, she didn't have the power to create another world where she lived alone and free from the burden of so many siblings, did she?

She laughed briefly at the idea of banning them all to eternal entrapment in Za's tomb, delighted that no one knew her precious secret: the one subtle diamond-shaped freckle on her chest right between her breasts that made her skin different and, thus, somehow more special to her. She loved it even if she was the only one who knew about it. Unfortunately, her pleasure with her uniqueness quickly passed, and she resumed her usual, insufferable sameness of mood.

Her shoulders slumped down, and her gaze locked firmly to the floor.

She kicked the jaguar fur robes to the side and yawned, exhausted by the thought of deciding which gown she would wear today, what jewels she would tolerate hanging from her thin, delicate neck during her daily dance for the queen. Even now, half-naked in her thin, wispy linen nightgown designed by her personal seamstress, she felt the weight of the extravagant accessories in her drawer, carat after carat, pull her down to the ground in disgust of her so-called life.

Screw this boring and terrible life, she thought, unable to find anything of merit amongst so many things in her immediate surroundings. She yearned for something simpler, some purpose worth holding on to. Some challenge, some grand adventure. Her shallow breath escaped her lips in defeat.

Her maids entered, eyes also peeled to the ground, determined to please her with their reverence. Little did they know, she would have much preferred one of them dared to speak with her and discuss trifle things like the sound streams made while the abundant fish nestled and protected their eggs, or the fineness of a gentle breeze across her cheek.

Instead, the obedient tripe kept their gaze down and did their jobs perfectly, just as everyone did here in the perfect world of Ardnyt.

She dropped to her rear on her lavish chaise and sighed. What she wouldn't give for an interesting day where someone screwed up something for the fun of it.

The maids laid out her three red gowns, their material smooth, full, and made of perfectly woven precious silk. Surprisingly odd was the source of such perfection: the protein fiber fibroin produced by the larvae of the mulberry silkworm, Bombyxharvested, reared in captivity, and tumbled around in a boiling pot of water to speed up their spooling rears, for just that purpose.

"Perfect material for such a perfectly boring life," the youngest Ivi princess said, and all the maids giggled with delight at her obvious pleasure of their efforts to help her dress like her sisters had always done before her.

How can this garment, spun from the youngest of boiling insects, possibly cover me and my secret desire to be unique and special in our expanding world growing warmer by the day as our sun slowly increases in size and purpose?

She shivered at the thought of the sun increasing in power, despite the heat on her skin. Her thoughts lingered on the word "purpose" and swirled there like she imagined the insect larvae might have while they formed this perfect thread.

She imagined the priceless silk thread swirling, changing colors, and becoming somehow even more valuable as it mingled with impurities and unintended minerals of color that might have accidently fallen into the vat instead of the purified hot water in the pot from which it actually came. The possibility of imperfections made the silk cloth seem so much more perfect to her.

The breeze, perhaps, or the sounds and smells in the air on a cool and unpredictable day might contaminate it in the most wonderful of ways. The very nature of other surrounding unknown imperfections infusing the fibers of the material so that it became more complex, yet simple simultaneously, as it swirled round her, all her family, and even the entire village in a slow, less deliberate way than their standard of maximum efficiency.

"Perhaps less is sometimes more," the princess said to one of the maids, Selen, a young thing who dared at the exact same time to catch and hold the princess's curious glance.

The chief maid pushed Selen aside and said, "Never. More

is always more, my lady." And like that, the matter was simply settled for all the staff in the room. Yet Azzå, the young princess, wasn't so sure. Some part of her knew less could also be more if the Norn Sisters of fate, or better yet, Nido, had willed it to be so.

Thankfully, most of the maids left her to her breakfast.

Just as she sat to eat... Flash! A cold draft filled the chamber, and her vision fluttered. Before her, just a few feet away, frozen water formed pointy spikes on the limbs of a crumbling old tree stump out front of shanty quarters, quarters that felt like more of a home than this grand bedchamber. Oddest of all, Selen was there, too, holding her hand and crying over some great loss they both had suffered.

The princess tried to remember the last time she lost something of value, but couldn't think of anything. Anything lost here was always immediately replaced with an exact or even better replica.

The vision passed, and she sighed, both with confusion about what had just happened and her overwhelming desire to step into that frozen drop of water and become internally iced to match it.

"Purpose. Everything has a bright, perfect, and summery purpose or it is surely never here, Azzå," she remembered someone say.

After placing her fingertips to her temples to stop the ceaseless chatter in her curious mind, the tenderhearted princess yawned and stretched her long and lanky legs. If she were one of her three older sisters, she would have been pissed to be up so early before the rest of her people. But she held a secret close to her core that other people just didn't have. She knew a thankful heart uncovered treasures amongst what other people would call garbage. And those gifts, the ones inside her, were worth more than anything that had ever existed outside of her.

So she thanked the flawless floor for letting her sweep it after the servants left...just for fun. She bowed to the golden beams above her head and promised to dust them later when no one was looking to thank them for holding up the weight of the slate roof. She pulled her arms in tight and clapped for the tapestries that told the legendary stories of old and swore she would read them out loud laterone by one, missing none, omitting none.

She cut out the softest center of her morning slice of cake, gave half to the blue-black wolf, and ate the crusted edges herself. Then she gave thanks for curiosity in her always hungry mind that demanded she try something different tomorrow but also kept her getting up each morning to keep her going.

"Stuffed is not such a bad thing if we can organize it somehow, Toby," she said. She laughed and shook her shoulders to mimic the creature. Unable to resist it any longer, a simple song gathered in her throat and demanded she hum it out loud. She figured why bother holding it in so much. Only the closest servants, already sworn to secrecy, could hear her in the morning above the daily trumpets outside, anyway. She rolled her full hips to the rhythm of her made-up song while she danced about her grand room, making her best attempt to honor the limitless possessions she owned with some of her personal attention. The work she wasn't allowed to do as a princess felt good and strong and pure. Before long, the tune grew and grew until she realized she was singing quite loudly, and she laughed again.

But since Nido had damned her overflowing world to a lack of adventure or challenge, she decided she had better stop the momentum of her joy before the powerful Goddess struck the princess down by a bolt of lightening and killed her. She dropped her shoulders, shifted her weight to the right, and looked at the ground, searching for some misery to hold on to.

Quickly, she found itthe way her mother had died while giving birth to her and applied the mandatory mask of Ardnyt. Even she knew it was an act though; at any moment she could snap out of it by simply humming the tune, offering up her thanks for a few things. She allowed herself just one morsel of gratitudeher song and the sweet company it offered her in her cluttered life. And so she sang one more verse on the inside to shield her core from the pain she had to wear on the outside.

She then recited the morning's scripted prayer just as she had done all the mornings before this one for all of those who had already suffered enough to merit their death, thus, accomplishing a successful exit from a life supposedly made to teach some elusive and ever-changing lesson she had never quite figured out.

"Those we have lost from this life, may your souls finally find rest and peace below in Tyndra. May the cold earth feel refreshing on your toes, and may, unlike here where we are broken creatures so unworthy of Nido's mercy, Her joy meet your every step and bless you with the glory of Her undeserved forgiveness in your new place of adventure."

She knew the prayer was supposed to give her hope, but she hated saying it. It seemed to her she had been placed unwillingly in a game without being told the rules and then been punished for not being able to recognize the prize no one had shown her. As a child, she was told it offered her solace to know a higher power would grace her in a beautiful way, but somehow that never settled her deep inside. In fact, she considered that total absurdity, bordering on insulting, and definitely invalidating of her worth.

Briefly, she questioned Nido's will...but then thought better of the blasphemy when she remembered all the cruel things the Goddess was capable of, like allowing evil foxes to steal your children as punishment for some thing you didn't know you had done.

She quickly said the prayer again, remembering her place: to be an imprisoned and unassuming figurehead without any real power. Besides, she had an okay life. Better than most even. Who the heaven-of-Ardnyt was she to question and doubt and ask for something more interesting and exciting than what she already had? Asking for more adventure was greedy, and she might be punished for that.

"Forgive me, Nido," she said, slumping her shoulders down and making her breath shallow and her body motionless. Her whispers sounded so low and foreign she wondered whose voice was coming out her pinched lips.

She really wanted adventure, struggle, a mission to accomplish with inherent value. A challengethat was what she wanted most of all. *Do not ask for more than your purpose in this life, you stupid child.*

Purposeshe considered the meaning of the word: the reason for which something was done or created.

Surely everything had a purpose, right?

What is my purpose then? To suffer, probably.

As far as she was concerned, suffering was an option. Painperhaps not. But the feeling of powerlessness to do anything about the pain that caused the sufferingyes. *Screw you, suffering. I am not trapped; you just think I am.*

Toby came back for one more trip around the room, and the princess quickly corrected herself.

"I am not bored. I have Toby and all the adventures we shall make together, even if it's a secret," she said and pulled her shoulders back up straight and certain.

But Azzå still didn't know her greater purposethe one deeper and more significant than dancing for her aunt, the queen, round the Irminsul, three times to the right and then three times to the left.

She imagined the prized objectthe Irminsul, a symbol of Nido's promise to protect her people.

"Oh we need you now, Nido. Where are you? And why have you forsaken us? Do you not love your children?" she asked and dropped her chest slightly.

The Irminsul: a thick staff at least six feet high made from the pure white tusk of some monstrous creature that had once roamed these lands. The top portion, measuring a foot or so across, was forged of flawless, impenetrable steel and shaped like the span of a fine bird's powerful wings. A delicate silver inscription had been carved by some unknown hand in a circular pattern down the length of the pole which ended in a metal cup that bore its way deep into the earth to hold the pole upright against gravity.

She pretended to spin round the grand column, hoping Nido might hear her prayer more clearlythree full twirls to the right, then the left.

As her feet carried her one way, away from the pleasures of tending to her home and Toby, her mind swirled there still. Unconsciously, her grandmother's incantation flowed like music through her mind in preparation for the dance always performed by the youngest of the women of the Ivi clan.

"*Twirl the Irminsul of Ardnyt,*
Which pierces truth with heat.
Locked in the vines of the Ivy Wall,
Two fates, each soul ought meet."

She heard Kirnéh, captain of the queen's guards, from the drawbridge singing her name, his obvious affection for her so nauseating, and considered running back home. Thankfully, she didn't.

Chapter Thirteen

EYES TO THE GROUND, she walked slowly, but not too slowly, in response to the captain's unreasonable demands that she give him her attention. It seemed like he wanted something from her, yet she just didn't know what.

"You are early like always, Princess Ivi," he said, bowing as she walked past.

Azzå looked at the timepiece above the painting of Ardnyt's strikingly handsome queen and smiled. There were no words to describe the queen's beauty. It was almost like it hovered above and around her, as if it belonged to something outside and beyond her, like a magic spell formed some external source of ethereal beauty.

Azzå shook the thought away and focused on the tyme. *Not early just in tyme.*

Kirnéh rushed to Azzå's side to grasp her hand. "Let me assist you, my favorite of all the princesses of Ardnyt. It would be my honor."

She groaned. His help was the last thing she wanted or needed. Help was for the weak. "No, thank you," she replied with a curtsy, but instead of averting her eyes like a princess should, she locked firmly on his for effect.

"But…"

"But I am perfectly capable of finding my Aunt Cassac's quarters to perform today's dance. I've been there more than once, you know."

He stammered like a fool. "But…but, my lady…" The nervous and devastatingly devoted captain searched his mind trying to find a reason, any reason to be of service to her. Even he had to admit his crush on her was out of control, but he couldn't find the strength to stop himself there. "May I…may I"

"No, you may not."

"May I hold the Irminsul for you while you dance, please?"

Before she had the chance to deny him once more, Azzå heard her aunt shout. Surprised by the urgency of the request, she dropped her white glove.

Delighted for the excuse to do something of value for the object of his affection, Kirnéh bent over to grab it. That was when Azzå saw his mark.

She gasped, her eyes as wide as the thick glass between heaven and hell.

Oh my Nido! It cannot be!

The mark was red, not blue-black, yet undeniably the same shape from her dream that matched the one on her chest, the same damn onea diamond at the nape of this groveling idiot's neck. *You have to be kidding me. How is this possible?*

Despite the heat in the room, chills coursed down her spine like a flurry of snowflakes to the core of her nervous system, and she suddenly realized that at least twice, maybe too many times to count, she had been here in this moment before.

A thought that felt foreign, yet also familiar, swam through her mind. *Will we see the truth in him this tyme? It's our last chance to find a way out.*

The queen screamed once more, and Azzå jumped. This time she said, "Yes. Come with me, Kirnéh. Come now."

"Yes Miss," he replied, grinning like a child.

Chapter Fourteen

"DANCE. Dance now. We must maintain our half of the globe," the queen demanded. "Lock it back in place. I am losing…"

"Yes, my Aunt," Azzå said, quite confused by the queen's words. Lately, the queen had seemed distracted on more than one occasion, absent even. Worse than that, nervous, and she kept saying odd things like, *"Our half."*

"Kirnéh, hold the Irminsul while she twirls. Hold it strong. Hold it steady. Maybe it will keep the divide…" The queen, obviously less than convinced they would succeed, looked to the side and clenched her jaw.

"Yes, my Lord," the captain said, groveling.

"Maybe there is a bit of tyme left yet. For us to…" The queen took a deep breath and brought her attention back to the large staff.

Just then, another guard rushed in, chest heaving, and dropped his hands on his knees while he gathered all the air he could. "The foxes, my Lord. The creepy fox thingsthey have stolen another child and forced it into the Ivy Wall. We couldn't capture the horrid creature. It flew like… I know you will think I'm nuts, but the nasty thing flew away, just like an eagle, once the child was ensnared in the vines. We shot it at, and it kept going despite the bloody wounds."

"There will be no stopping the fox animals now," the queen said.

"More than foxes. These were mutants," the guard declared.

"Combinations of animal parts just like…just like a beast?" Kirnéh asked.

"Like the Enfield," the guard replied, backing up and trying to get away.

Azzå stopped twirling. "A monstrous beast like in the fairy-tale? Ridiculous."

The queen covered her mouth and mumbled something.

"Say it's not true," Azzå demanded. "This guard is obviously hallucinating. Fairytales aren't real. Everyone with half a brain knows they are just stupid stories to scare us."

"Not the story of Za, I'm afraid," she said. "And our Goddess, Nido, has decided her patience with this lesson in tyme is over. It has begun." The queen sighed and sat down.

"What?" Azzå said.

"The end of tyme. If only…we would have had a chance. But dark magic is dark, after all."

Just as the queen said the confusing words, the Irminsul cracked right down the middle. Kirnéh tried to hold it together, but there was no way. In his very hands, it dissolved, and half of it disappeared into thin air.

Everyone gasped. Everyone but Azzå, who dropped to the ground, half of her strength stolen as if the other part of her had dissolved into thin air along with the Irminsul.

Kirnéh released what remained of the staff and ran to the girl's side. He scooped up her fragile body and rushed her to the queen's bed. Anyone could see his affection, his devotion, and his eternal service to the princess.

Painfully, the scar on the back of neck went ice cold and he hollered.

"Don't bother checking," the queen said. "The scar has frozen now. You have probably lost your final chance to convince her of your innocence."

Azzå's head rolled back as she lost consciousness. Her pulse was low and dropping. Her fingers, like her lips, turned blue.

"She's so cold. How is that possible?" the captain said. "What do you mean, my innocence?"

"Yes, so cold," the queen said and shook her head.

"Is she dying?" Kirnéh begged the queen, demanding the one answer that no one had to give him. Tenderly, he laid her down on the elegant, golden, goose-down comforter and moaned.

"I cannot say if she will die, not for sure, yet. Do you not know Za's legend?"

"Parts of it. It's just a story."

"Is it? Are you sure?"

"I'm not sure of anything except that I would die for this girl. I've felt that way since the first tyme I laid eyes on her."

"I know. I remember. And you have, too many tymes to count" the queen replied and laughed nervously. "But the problem is she doesn't know that, does she?" The Queen Cassac paced the room, her thoughts light-years and universes away.

"No. I have never been brave enough. She has no idea how I feel about her."

"You two. Always the same problem."

"Excuse me?"

"You never say. She always assumes. Idiots, both of you."

He was too confused to reply.

"I will make an appeal to Nido for one last chance," the

queen declared. "But it is futile. There is no turning back. The Ivi has hours to decide, at most, which of our two worlds will survive. If we lose the battle for Azzå's attention and this side of her divided will, then we lose everything, and our world dies with her body."

"Then I will fight for her."

"Fighting is good. The truth of your eternal devotion is better."

"Whomever I must fight. I will lead the army wherever I must go. No matter how far," Kirnéh said. His declaration was met with cheers.

"But what about the mutant fox things?" Emilio asked.

"We will defeat them, too."

"They were unaffected by bullets."

"We will get bigger guns and go wherever we must. Even through the Ivy Wall with all its monsters and straight into hell," Kirnéh claimed.

"Even in to Tyndra?" Emilio asked, trembling. "But that is a terrible place. Full of suffering and pain."

The queen smiled. Now they were getting somewhere. Sacrifices were at the heart of this matter to begin with, after all. "Yes. That is true. But if Tyndra wins, we lose. Only one world will remain when the Gods are finished teaching us this lesson."

"Then to Tyndra we march, " Kirnéh said, far more bravely than he felt.

The queen stared into space and shook her head. "The truth is the only thing that can help us now. It's also the only thing that can set you and this little spirited one free," she said, pointing to Azzå.

In the distance, the blue foxes howled high-pitched screams in perfect unison to claim their final prize: the end of tyme in Ardnyt.

Section III: The War

Won't lovers revolt now?
    No, it is opposition…
    Murder for a jar of red rum.

Draw, O coward.
    Name now one man!

O, stone, be not so…
    Stop! Murder us not, tonsured rumpots.
    Draw no dray a yard onward!

Sworn I sit, 'tis in rows…
    Draw pupil's lip upward-
    Never odd or even.

Reviled did I live, said I, as evil I did deliver.
    He won snow, eh?
    No witness, a fool. A nasal aria's time emits air. Alas, an aloof assent: I won.

Chapter Fifteen

FOR MANY DAYS, a great battle was waged across the Ivy Wall. On one side, the swirling black-blue side of the wall, terrible fires raged and burned all available life to the ground. On the other, the orange-red side, cruel showers of mounting ice and snow fell from above as everything cold and horrible in the skies fell to thwart the efforts of the men who fought so bravely.

The oddest part of the affair was that both sides had no idea who or what exactly they were fighting. Honestly, they didn't even know what they were fighting for besides the safe return of their children. The babies, frozen inside the wall, had become part of the structure of vines entangling the wall, inseparable and enmeshed within.

Most likely, the little one were already dead, the first wave of massive casualties to come.

As the battle raged, droves of animals came from inside the Ivy Wall to stand guard at the borders. Many appeared to be a fox from one side but resembled a wolf from another angle, sometimes seemingly blue and others red. Occasionally, one would call out with the cry of an eagle or the roar of a lion. And although it seemed odd the same creatures that had stolen the children would stand beside their motionless bodies without eating or attacking them, that was exactly what happened. The soldiers were convinced it was to keep the bodies of the children protected against the battle for their own rabid consumption later.

They couldn't have been more wrong.

Each effort to win from one side was matched with equal vigor from the other. More guns on one side meant more guns on the other. The same for the canons, the tossed boulders, the arrows.

Fire fell from the sky and burned the ground on one side of the wall as ice fell from the sky to freeze it on the other. Nowhere was safe except inside the wall where none of the weapons reached but appeared to pass though, like magic, directly onto the other side.

Chapter Sixteen

IN TYNDRA:

Unable to make progress against the other side, unable to locate the king, and unable to make sense of the unexplainable situation, Henrik turned to the only thing left to him in a tyme like this: his magic crystal ball.

As he looked into his glass ball, a gift handed down through the ages from the descendants of Athena herself, he saw a vision despite the blizzard surrounding him. He fell back, unable to believe what was before him. At first, he blamed it on coincidence, on bad luck, on anything other than the insanity he witnessed.

Every arrow sent into Ardnyt reached back into Tyndra perfectly matched.

For hours he watched this phenomenon before he considered the impossible as possible. As more warriors prepped for the next tier of battle, Henrik shared his observation with Azza.

"It is as if we are fighting ourselves. It's something from a cruel fairytale. How can that be possible?" he said, shaking his head at the absurdity coming from his own lips.

"What do you mean?"

He shook his head again obviously afraid to say anything more. "Well. Hmm. You're going to think this is crazy, but…"

"Go on," she encouraged. Truth be told, she had considered telling him she had this crazy little idea about fairytales herself. That somehow her story was related to Za's. But that was just too crazy to say out loud. She didn't want to lose him now.

He sighed and paused before saying, "It's as if there are two versions of each of us: one in Tyndra and another in Ardnyt. It's like we are fighting ourselves."

She just looked at him.

He laughed nervously, trying to reclaim the words once they had been spoken.

She shrugged. "Maybe not so crazy. I've been thinking that…" Again, she almost told him her ridiculous theory about Za but backed down at the last minute, terrified Henrik would reject her for such self-inflated absurdity. Could he love a woman with delusional thoughts? Probably not. No, certainly not.

She cleared her head of thoughts about Za and tried to listen, but it was hard to focus on his words with so much swirling around insider her mind.

He explained, best as he could, what he had seen in the crystal ball. Eventually he handed it to her.

"Oh," she said, at first just for support but then in genuine surprise. "I see what you are talking about."

"Crazy."

"Crazy." It was just like something magical, some odd spell out of one her fairytale books. She loved fairytales. But a real one? Real magic? Dark magic? Some kind of spell? Was that even possible?

The longer she stared, the more fear gripped her heart.

Every arrow returned an arrow.

Every cannon, a cannon.

Every advance, matched in perfect symmetry.

Every death…

"It can't be true!" Azza cried. "How can we possibly win?"

"We can't." He shook his head. "We can only lose this tyme."

For the rest of the morning, she observed the battle through Athena's precious gift to one of the first founders of Tyndra, and there was no denying the obvious: there was no way to win this war. It was a war from within. A dark and terrible spell had ruined their only chance to survive, and no one would save the children.

Azza lay down in one of the soldiers' tents, shaking. She told Henrik she planned to gather her thoughts and think of another way out of this war and out of the storm. But the truth was she was trying to find a way to gather the strength to tell the others. The children were lost. Tyndra was lost. They were going to die.

If they fought the other side, they killed themselves. As the storm worsenednow the worst she had ever seen in her lifethey were as good as dead. If not from exposure, surely over tyme, starvation would claim them.

Talby had not left the warmth of Azza's sweater in hours, but now he climbed up to the head of the cot and howled a deafeningly high-pitched scream in painful mourning. He understood exactly how she felt and tucked his tail in defeat while he marched back and forth at the head of the cot with palpable anxiety.

Not until after Azza's swollen, tear-stained eyes had closed did he risk sitting down to rest. A few moments later, Azza's eyes rolled back into her head. Her body, from a sudden rush of internal heat, shook violently, and with one seizure-like twitch, her total awareness left her trembling body behind in Tyndra.

Chapter Seventeen

IN ARDNYT:

Azza awakened, terribly disoriented by the rush of hot air surrounding her. She felt lost but somehow found.

She stopped trembling and opened her eyes in a much more fragile version of a body that she knew, yet didn't, on a grand and golden bed instead of the cot upon which she had lain.

"Talby? Talby?" she called.

She searched the room frantically for any sign of her friend. Movement caught her attention as a blue wolf skulked out of the corner. She should have been afraid the creature was going to eat her, but he was just so small and cute. Moreover, the adorable little thing averted his eyes in submission. This was no monster. Besides, there was no tyme for fear; people she knew and loved, like Henrik, were dying.

Oh my Odin, I do love Henrik. I love him. And I think he loves me, too.

She smiled despite their imminent death and demanded of the wolf, "Who are you, and what do you want?"

The beautiful puppy rushed to her side and rubbed against

the bed, wagging his tail in delight just like Talby did. Almost like it knew her and knew her well.

She could still hear the screams and battle sounds in the background but wouldn't give into the fear. There wasn't enough tyme.

She checked her body, part by part, to figure out if she was alive or dead. *Good. Alive. I think good, anyway.* She traced her chest, just to be sure. Her mark was the same: a subtle diamond. It was the same mark that matched the one behind the boy's neck in her dream, and Henrik's neck adorned the symbol as well.

She loved him, the very man she used to hate. The same man she thought she would never forgive and could never possibly understand. And here was a blue wolf she didn't know who acted as though she should.

What could it all possibly mean?

Still dizzy from the extreme heat and the effort of admitting she had to figure out this puzzle or concede to death, she climbed down the golden bed and walked around the room in utter confusion.

She stumbled from one heavy and luxurious piece of furniture to the next. Never had she seen such colors. The materials were so shiny and thick she could hardly tolerate not touching everything around her. The horrible heat drenched her in a wetness she had never known under her arms, behind her neck, and at her waistline.

Her clothes were thick and heavy, which seemed ridiculous to her. She could have used these heavy layers when she was cold. Now these things were a nuisance, an unnecessary burden of luxury no one who lived in this kind of dripping and insufferable heat would ever need.

Slowly at first, then steadily increasing in urgency, she stripped the layers. *Screw this under skirt.* Heavy beads round her neckgorgeous but absurd. *You have to be kidding me.* How could they have served a purpose other than to bother her?

A purpose. Ah! The idea haunted her. She wondered what the purpose was of her awareness in an identical, but finer yet more burdened, version of herself. She came from hell. She knew only of two worlds: the hell-of-Tyndra and the heaven-of Ardnyt. This was not Tyndra. Was it possible?

Was this place Ardnyt?

If so, how could it have felt like a larger burden than the ultimate burden in hell? *Maybe Tyndra wasn't so bad. Maybe the hell-of-Tyndra was a misnomer.*

She checked in the mirror. Yes, she looked the same, only thinner and frailer with a long, thick rope of hair braided down her back, high-arched eyebrows, a firm and full lip, and prominent collarbones. *Yep, I'm me. Only I'm not, am I?*

Then she remembered the glass ball. The duality. The two perfectly matched but upside down worlds. *Am I on the other side?*

Holy spell of insanity. Was it possible?

She gasped in fear. Some type of spell had trapped her away from Henrik, away from Talby, away from everything she knew or cared about.

Cold wasn't so bad. Not in comparison.

The thought pinged through her brain and slapped her*in comparison.*

She wiped the horrible sweat off her brow and growled as she scurried around the room, trying to make sense of this place.

A regal woman entered and whispered Azza's name in an exotic, but not displeasing, accent. When Azza didn't respond, the womana wise expression radiating from her flawless, ethereally beautiful face stood back and observed.

"You?" the woman asked.

She nodded.

"I see…"

After watching the girl flitter back and forth, distinctly lacking the grace of a fine dancer who spins round the Irminsul, the older, infinitely gorgeous woman spoke. "I see, my dear, that you have found yourself out of place."

Iced at her core, yet melting in comparison, Azza turned round to face the regal woman.

"Welcome to Ardnyt, child. You and yours will have passed through the Ivy. Incredible. I never expected that."

Azza glared at the woman, ready to attack if she proved an enemy. Could someone so strikingly beautiful be an enemy?

The wolf growled and paced back and forth between them.

"Toby loves you instantly," the queen said and laughed while watching from a distance. "Of course you are fine. Amazing. Look at you, whole and complete. But thirsty. You must be famished and so, so thirsty."

Azza shook her head.

The queen gave her water and smiled. "I remember the first tyme I crossed. It was terrible. And I was so thirsty." She laughed once more. "My mind picked Ardnyt. Unfortunately, the rest of me picked Tyndra." The queen looked at the floor in obvious pain. "I do miss him, you know."

Her suspicions confirmed she was in Ardnyt, Azza replied. "It seems so. And you? Do I know you? Are you good or bad? Will you hurt me?"

The queen laughed. "I'm good as far as I am concerned. But even villains think they are good. Did you know that? And besides, some of my people might argue that point after the last tax was imposed." She laughed again.

"Who are you? No wait, I don't care? Who am I?"

"That is always the most interesting question, my child. Good for you. Profound questions always merit profound answers. Thus, I'll answer them both, and you can figure out how true my answers are. Here in Ardnyt they call me Queen. And I call this version of you niece."

A man who looked almost identical to Henrik rushed through the door and squealed with delight that Azza was up on her feet. His pleasure at her healthy condition, so palpable it coated the room, dripped off the ceiling just like the sweat under Azza's arms.

Azza gasped at the coincidence. Then she remembered it wasn't coincidence. It was…*in comparison.*

The queen added, "And we call him Kirnéh. He is captain of my guards, of course. He is strong and valiant here but treats you with reverent and blubbering affection, just as you might expect."

In comparison.

"I see," said Azza, stumbling backwards from the implosion of her reality. And suddenly, for the first time ever, she actually did see. She saw *in comparison.*

Chapter Eighteen

With immeasurable grief, Henrik leaned over the lifeless body of Azza Ivi. He held her hand with the fine devotion, almost obsession, of an unrequited lover who considered himself unworthy of her touch. Yet he was unable to walk away. Without the promise of Azza's survival, he had nothing left to fight for.

His next in command kept asking for the next orders. He never answered.

The snow fell in sheets so deep and furious that the visibility outside made worse into terrible. The soldiers had lost all hope. The people had lost all hope. The children were trapped in the Ivy Wall, and there was nothing anyone could find worth fighting for. They had all given up.

With longing, Henrik grasped his sword. "If you would just say goodbye, I would fall on my blade. Why won't you answer me? Where are you? Did the magic infect you and steal you from me? What has happened? Azza, give me hope or I shall die from the pain of you not answering me."

He made a decision: in the morning, he would walk into

open battle and offer up his own life to speed up the process and lessen the suffering of them all. He sent out the message for all who wanted to join him to consider massive suicide to stop the pain and start the crossing over. Ah to trade the hell-of-Tyndra for the-heaven-of-Ardnyt, finally awaiting them as they crossed to the other side. The only possible answer was a quick suicide induced trip to salvation or a slow, terribly unnecessary and painful death. Two very different routes to the same place. Why wait to die in battle? Why take the long road when suicide was so much quicker, so much more efficient?

Chapter Nineteen

IN ARDNYT:

"Why have they stopped fighting?" Azza asked and set down the glass ball, an exact replica of the ball she had held with Henrik.

The queen shrugged.

"I don't understand. What is Henrik doing?"

"He's giving up on you. Just like always."

"What?"

"Never underestimate the power of the will of humanity. Without it, humans are just another species, no different than that wolf, or the squirrel, or the deer. Look at your captain. He's already dead inside. His eyes are empty pits of no value now. Thus, his people are doomed, too. Tyndra's precious King Cassac is gone. Ha! Your God's promise of protection via the Irminsul splintered in two. The captain useless. Tyndra's children helplessly trapped in the Ivy Wall with a monstrous beast. Just like ours. It is over."

"But... What if?"

"What can you possibly do? You are weak."

"Never."

"You always have been. So weak."

Azza nodded. She was weak. Wasn't she?

Inside, the queen smiled, but she kept her face a flat mask of apathy. "With the power of will, we had a chanceno battle is too hard, no mountain too high, no answer too difficult to find. But now…"

"Both sides have given up. Will no one find the answer?"

"I might have asked you the same question if I didn't know that you are so weak?"

"But you are the queen!"

"Am I? Have I ever really ruled this place? Perhaps someone's willful ways are the true source of this dilemma?" The queen's mask cracked momentarily before she reapplied it.

"Tell me what to do? I'll do"

"You must be willing to do the unthinkable, the very thing you have never been able to do. Otherwise…"

"Tell me. Show me!" Azza demanded.

"Perhaps it is tyme to learn what you have already done?" The Queen Cassac pointed to an old text sitting upon a grand book display case. The title *The Girl Who Imprisoned Tyme,* by the Brothers Grimm.

"But?"

"Go on," the queen encouraged. "You might say, this tyme, it is now or never."

Chapter Twenty

WHILE AZZA READ the prophetic text, the Monarch Cassac made her final decision to remain as queen in Ardnyt. The people here in the heaven-of-Ardnyt needed her more than the warriors in Tyndra needed their demented king. It was no revelation to her that the conditions in the hell-of-Tyndra made the people there harder by nature, far cleverer, and much sturdier of spirit in their souls. The souls in the heaven-of-Ardnyt had never suffered. They wouldn't transition to whatever came next for them with grace. They obviously needed her considerably more than Tyndra needed him. She loved the idea of seeing that firsthand.

She waved her hand before her heart and sealed the pact that what remained of her soul would persist in this physical structureboth halves of her yin and yang reunited once again and forever more as the possibility of the lessons of duality slipped away from her for the last tyme. Her energy always just slightly more feminine than masculine to begin with, queen had always suited her better than king. Who needed a prince to become the queen after all?

Not a Saccas, not a Cassac either.

Surely, this was her proof if she would ever have any.

The queen, feeling so strong and whole again, risked a subtle glance at Azza, such a curious and amusing creature, and smiled. Azza would be the next to choose. Or maybe even the last? Who knew other than Odin anyway? Nido, that's who. For a moment, she paused to consider which part of God she liked better: Nido, the feminine or Odin, the masculine. Did the two sides cancel each other out or augment one another? She couldn't be sure. Thankfully didn't really care.

The queen touched her fingernail and thanked it for the unexpected gift it had given her. The chance to travel with awareness from one side of the ultimate duality to other was a priceless gift, one that offered perspective, so rare in days such as these, when no one seemed to value anything much. It was a gift to have a chance to observe the outcome of this lesson first-hand: as above, so below. *In comparison.*

Chapter Twenty-One

AZZA RUSHED OVER to the great text and examined the covermost likely centuries old. When she opened the book with extreme and reverent caution, an odd, yet slightly familiar scent took her briefly back to a memory she couldn't completely recall. She scanned the table of contents and found the right chapter. Certain the memory would come to her soon enough, she turned to the proper sectionright in the middle.

The Girl Who Imprisoned the World in Tyme

Once upon a time, there was born a quartet of intriguing girls, each an incarnation of destiny and life itself, with very special, yet potentially deadly gifts. And as the four sisters had no mother and no father to speak of and were innately able to wield such powerful magic, they were placed directly under the guardianship of Odinmaster of their universe. He called them Sisters of the Norns and placed them in the greater service of the good of his domain which he ruled in a fair, but oft' misunderstood, way.

Determined to mold the Norns' natural gifts in a positive manner, Odin assigned them each an honorable task with respect to time. The first and most beautiful sister, Urtha, was made responsible for managing memories of the past. The second and most charming, Vertha, was made responsible for the present moment. And the thirdthe most creative of the quartet, Skulda, was made responsible for the future. But the youngest, a spirited and often distracted creature named Za, refused to be made responsible for anything as complicated as time. Thus, to keep her out of the way of the other three, Odin assigned her the simple task of wasting time.

And so while her sisters served humanity under Odin's guidance, Za played and dreamed and played some more.

One day, while walking with a sweet little lamb, Za stumbled upon a demigod named Ehnrik and fell instantly in love with his half-human, half-god's smile. Unfortunately, he was even more prone to distraction than she was, which was definitely saying something...

Even though their affection was mutual, some scheme by one or the other was always ruining things for them. Like the time he bought some magic beans and was almost killed by a jealous giant for his golden egg. Or the time Za dared a pair of clever elves to try to teach a senile old couple how to properly make shoes despite their total incompetence at any task of significance. Or when she put a whole village to sleep whilst finding some poor prince willing to do just about anything in exchange for the chance to slay a magical dragon. His reward for victory, of course, to wake the rescued princess with love's first kiss only to discover he had been tricked into kissing a man disguised as a woman.

However, most painful of all by far, the time Ehnrik agreed to help Urtha, the eldest of the Norns, secretly wed the honorable and handsome Prince of the Netherlands before he was forced to wed the monarch of a neighboring land famous for harboring witches, specifically a terrible old witch named Saccas. To compound such horror, the Prince's betrothed bride had a face more like a beast's than a beauty, and the groom, a good man who believed marriage should be anchored by love not duty, had always secretly loved Urtha, eldest of the Norns.

Ehnrik, who sympathized with the prince's misfortune, facilitated the negotiations that led to Urtha's acceptance of the prince's sudden proposal. And if the marriage could possibly be consummated before the event planned the following morning, any subsequent weddings would be invalid in Odin's eyes. But just before the covert vows were uttered, something terrible came to pass. The ghastly other woman, who turned out to be an evil sorceress, the Saccas herself, with schemes of her own, stole the prince's handsome face and exchanged it with her own once beastly mug.

When Urtha removed her veil and saw her groom's altered, ghastly face, she collapsed in shock. Enhrik, certain that love's first kiss could undo the witch's spell, carried Urtha's devastated body into the prince's bedchamber for a chance to undo what had happened. The evil witch, still not done with her meddling, captured the image of Enhrik carrying the unconscious bride with a magical piece of glass and used it to deceive Za. The witch, now beautiful beyond measure, claimed Enhrik had done unthinkable things to Urtha's body with Odin's permission and then offered it up to a hideous monster that had surely eaten it to destroy the evidence of their crime against the Sisters of the Norns.

Harnessing all the power of hate within her heart as retribution, Za destroyed the power of love's first kiss by giving it rules and conditions and turned the beast's gardens into ropes of thick ivy, as complicated as her new rules of love, with which to imprison him for all eternity. Now just another fool to the witch's lies, Za locked herself in her family's tomb so no one alive could find her and make her face what had happened.

But worst by far, in order to spread her pain through every

corner of the mutable universe, Za took one of Odin's most prized possessions, his snow globe, with her into the darkness of a time without the possibility of the past. Why? Because her sister Urtha, weaver of the past memories, was gone forever.

Za called this new existence "tyme" and vowed to waste it all.

Legend has it to this day that having forgotten how to break her own terrible spell, Za remains there yet, trapped in a tomb of her own making, staring into the globe, trapped in a tyme of her own making, unable to remember what happened to the past. Now more a part of the globe than not, the glass ball has become her guilty prison on every levelas above, so below.

Because she has no memories of the past, she does not even recognize the face of her Enhrik. Every day since, he has been trying to convince her of his innocence by the diamond-shaped mark behind his neck during the few moments between awake and sleeping when his spirit visits hers just before she rises each morning.

She read as fast as she could through the first several pages in total disbelief yet complete acceptance.

In that moment, she remembered everything. Oh how she remembered it all: her sisters, the Norns. *Poor, poor Urtha*. The past memories of all her prior lives all had been lost. The unintended effects of her evil spell that had trapped them in this existence called tyme. The witch's beautyflawless except for a horrid fingernail on her left hand. Even the witch's cackle as Za spoke her terrible vows made of hate. She saw it all so clearly–the beast that ate her sister, the wall she made to entrap him, the globe she imprisoned in her tomb.

She thought of her name: Azza Ivi.

Oh how life had been trying to tell the truth for so long. Za backwards plus Za forwards was Azza. Ivi was the same forwards and backwards and just one letter different than the ivy of the ivy wall. Awestruck, she laughed nervously at all the clues she had overlooked for so long. And her lover Enhrik… she turned the letters round in her mindHenrik and Kirnéh. How had she missed something so obvious? The letters forwards and backwards or even just mixed up a bit always seemed to mean the same thing despite the difference in their order. *In comparison.*

She thought of both her first and last names once more, Azza Ivi. Then she remembered her innate power. She was a Norn, after all, full of magic. With all the force of her power and focused intention, she wished to return to Tyndra to find him, to tell him, to forgive him and undo what she had done, to see the face of love, to feel love's first kiss.

But would it be enough?

Even though she couldn't have explained how she did it, in a flash, she left Ardnyt and returned to her other trembling body in Tyndra.

But the last thing she heard was a familiar cacklethat, in fact, of a wicked witch, the Witch Saccas.

Chapter Twenty-Two

IN TYNDRA:

Azza awoke on the thin and frozen bed and knew she had made it back to Tyndra. Quickly, she stretched her limbs so exhausted by their disuse while she was in that fragile version of her body in Ardnyt. Talby growled to greet her, and she laughed. Then they both ran out to find Henrik, and if he was still alive, Azza planned to kiss him before the witch had the chance to kill them all.

Chapter Twenty-Three

IT DIDN'T TAKE LONG. Azza followed the screams and found Henrik on the battlefield near death like so many of the others. Spikes of ice filled the sky and rained down on them like frozen knives made of hate.

The wolves marched along the perimeter openly attacking soldiers who tried to get anywhere close to the Ivy Wall, the vines and fronds now frozen, too.

Many of the vines had turned to a pale brown ice; the wall was dying.

Henrik had lost blood and, from the state of his clothes, a lot of it.

She rushed over to him as he stumbled to the ground under a wall of ice, now turned maroon from the color of his spilled heme. He had slit his own wrists.

"I wanted to come to you in death. I was trying to find you in Ardnyt. I knew you were already there."

"Fool."

"Fool for you, yes."

Instantly, she remembered how completely she loved him. How long she had loved him. How much she had missed him.

She vowed not to waste any more of his or her tyme.

"I'm here. I will help you. I can help us all. Now I know. Love's first kiss."

He tried to laugh but couldn't. He was too weak, too far gone in his dying.

"Kiss me, damn it. I love you. I remember now. The mark, the spell, all of it."

He whispered, "Love has always been the most powerful spell. Why didn't we remember that sooner? Then I wouldn't have lived to die; I would have died to live."

"Maybe you just did."

She inhaled the scent of hima satiating fragrance so thick and delicious that it dripped off of him and filled her like no amount of milk ever had. This substance was luxurious and full of richness like milk's most delicious gift, creamy butter. For sure this was the smell of the lovely substancerich, yet light and slippery with its hold on you.

She thought of all the forms of love she had known in her lifeher sisters, her grandmother, even for her missing and probably dead King Cassac. None of them compared to this buttery love, of the delight, of the flavor of being this close to such a delicious man even if they were both about to die from the terrible storm.

Henrik, unable to resist the temptation, licked his lips. Now his oily flavor had baked the frozen insides of him, wafted up the vents of his spirit, spread to her, and then dripped back down to coat him once more. He smiled at the thought of the warmness inside her despite their imminent death, and she wondered how he had the strength, in a moment like this, to do anything but simply breathe.

Again unable to resist, she drew in a mouthful of his scent. Or was it hers? She was no longer able to tell the difference of where his flavor ended and hers began. His musk, her pheromonesnow one intermingled aroma of passionately churning connection. The conjoined fragrance, so powerful and intoxicating, burned the inside of her frozen mouth and melted the ice that used to be her throat.

She inhaled deeply, taking it all in: the heat, the smell, the liquid, the desire, now the steam of them melting the sheets of ice all around them. She tried to hold on to it: the pain of turning her inside from solid, meaningless layers of ice into an uncontainable, ill definable, eternal gas. She shook her head no, with an undeniable *yes*, but there was just too much of him, or was it her, to hold on to.

Just to keep from dying from the overdose of this addictive substance, she swirled the mist of their passion down her lungs and through every cell in her body bathing herself in the drug of their mixture. Like a vice, it gripped her lower abdomen and took up residence in her pelvis, now throbbing and swelling with an urge of openness to receive even more of him.

But because there was no tyme for such a tempting and distracting thought in a critical moment like this, she blew her breath out quickly to force it back towards him. She wasn't sure which one of them needed her breath more.

The smile in his deeply sunken black eyes flashed wildly blue for a moment, the same blue as the boy's eyes from her reoccurring dream. He was the boy of her dreams; he always had been.

The truth of her thoughts lit the mark on the back of his neck from the inside, branding him hers, and her his forever.

He took the precious air from the space between them, their mixed air, and held on to it with all of his intensity. "Azza," he whispered. "I"

She knew better than to let his foolish words get in the way and ruin this moment, so she simply held her finger over his lips and pressed down lightly.

During a moment that lasted for all that was left of tyme, he held her gaze silently. Unable to remain separated from her, he moved into her and softly drew his lips upwards such that they stroked her finger.

His black eyes grew so large and bright that blue filled all the world around the two of them, trapped inside a sheet of ice that melted all tyme and space back into their last moment together.

Past became one with present and wrapped around all possible futures, and Azza knew tyme was about to end. "Kiss me, you fool," she uttered the invitation with the full force of her heart's intention.

"Yes?" he asked, more than affirmed. His body was so weak now that he fluttered in and out of what was real. Was this even happening, or was he already dead?

"Yes," she said, trying to keep him focused, certain the kiss would save him, would save them all, and put things right once more. "I forgive you. I don't understand why, but I choose to forgive you for what you did to my sister. I choose to love you instead of hate you."

She smiled, more with her eyes than her mouth, and leaned her lips firmly against the other side of that finger, that simple bone and flesh, that so easily traversable barrier between the very thing that would save them all: a full-hearted kissthe connection that would change everything for her, for him, for everyone.

Love's first kiss. Love, always the only infallible answer to every question anyone had ever asked. Could it really have been this simple? Could love's light and forgiveness shine away all darkness?

But did she, the source of the curse that birthed all this

suffering, deserve love's blessing? Did she deserve a chance to undo all the evil she had done? Did Henrik? Perhaps death was the more appropriate punishment. She was prepared to die in Henrik's place, ready to meet Odin, ready to bow at His feet and face her judgment day.

He paused now, confused by what she had just said. But did it matter now? Probably not. Certainly not.

He knew he was dying.

There was no surviving an injury this severe, but he would let her hold on to the illusion until he was past the point of no return. With his last few breaths, he would fill his lungs with the scent of her and know it had been a good life, one well worth living, and this, a death worth dying.

"When my eyes have lost final sight of the sun," he whispered, nudging her finger to the side to get that much closer to her lips, "you will still burn so brightly on my heart that I will see you forever more."

"Your wrists. Your neck. It's so much blood, but I know it will work, Henrik," she said with all the power she had left, and his name lingered like the karmic resonance of a thousand past lives on her full and throbbing lips.

"Cast me softly into hell with you," he added.

"We finally"

"Got it right." He smiled and moved closer still, knowing it would be the last tyme he moved this body.

Unable to stall any longer, she said, "I want to understand you, to choose you, to know every part of you."

"And I believe"he swallowed his last swallow"in something again."

"I would...I will...gladly take your place."

"I know you. I see you," he whimpered.

The goddess in him pulled forward the god in her and swirled them into one big mess of divine beauty.

Their trembling lips finally met as he closed his eyes, certain they wouldn't open again.

Azza was right; tyme stood in silent observance of the healing beauty of the moment because the hell-of-Tyndra had, even if only for this one moment, become the only heaven-of-Ardnyt the two of them had ever needed to know.

Chapter Twenty-Four

IN ARDNYT:

With the glass ball in her hand, the witch watched with great interest to see if the boy's eyes would open again.

"Surely not! Fairytales are stories invented by meddling little Norns." Her laugh, so shrill and terrible, sent all the mice scurrying out of the room.

Could love's first kiss really stop a spell that had served her so well for so long? After all, she was the queen, wasn't she? She was the king, too. And she never even had to wed that horrible Prince of the Netherlands. The same one who Za had trapped in the Ivy Wall on her behalf because the ignorant thing believed the bullshit story a beautiful witch had fed her about an image taken out of context.

"What a fool, you stupid little girl," the Witch Saccas said. She laughed, certain of exactly what to do next. She pulled out a black candle and lit a long and horrid nail on her smallest finger on fire with a match. Urgently, she carved several letters into the ebony wax while she imagined all the wrongs ever done unto her because of her ugly face. The same one now worn by Prince Enfield, ruler of mutant beasts. Despite her burning finger, she stared deeply into the raging flame while she said her nefarious incantation. Once the candle had sufficiently melted, she blew out the fire in her hand and dripped the hot wax on a small onyx stone, laughing sardonically while carving a second mark into the cursed wax.

Once the coal-black wax hardened on the stone's surface, she said these words: "From me back to you, my arrow strikes true. Say it with me Kirnéh."

Thousands of meters away on the battlefield in Ardnyt, a blank stare overtook Kirnéh's previously determined face. Streams of lava shot down from above. The fields were ablaze. His men were succumbing to their wounds too fast to measure. The pits of dead bodies grew and grew, but none of that mattered now. He had one last target to kill. The queen had said so. He had made her hold a black candle while she said it, and he would serve her until the very end. Then he could die like all the rest and hope for a better life on the other side of this world.

He pulled the arrow back as far as his chest muscles would allow and said the words Queen Cassac had demanded he utter when the tyme came for him to perform one last duty.

The tyme had come. He felt it in the deepest pits of his soul as if the devil itself made him do it.

"From me back on to you, my arrow take flight and might it strike true. On cursed winds, through bondage vinemark pain's truest source, the source of tyme."

Moments later, the queen's guard dropped to the ground and grabbed his chest in pain. The only sound he heard above his own muffled cries were that of a witch's wicked laugh.

Section IV: The Wall

In a regal age ran I.
   Revered now I live on. O did I do no evil, I wonder ever?
   Oh who was it I saw, oh who?

Flee to me, remote elf.
   Name now one man.
   Evil is a name of a foeman, as I live.

No, is Ivy's order a red rosy vision?
   No, it is open on one position.

Live not on evil...
   Now do I repay a period won?
   Now, sir, a war is won!

Chapter Twenty-Five

Azza ran as fast as she could, but there wasn't enough tyme left.

After the kiss, nothing had changed. Nothing for the better, anyway.

Love's first kiss was just a fairytale, one that she as Za herself had invented in one of her stupid attempts to waste tyme. Love never fixed anything.

Henrik never opened his eyes after their kiss, and the snow fell as fast as ever. In fact, it seemed to be getting worse. With every passing moment, another soul in Tyndra died thinking that life in Ardnyt would be better. They were dying for nothing. There was no better place to go. It was all the same place...*in comparison*

Why?

There was no other life in Ardnyt; it was just another side, another version of this same life. The people were already partially in Ardnyt, just unaware of the duality of their parallel existences. She saw that now. Dying did nothing to change the lesson she had to learn for them all. Learning the lesson was what mattered, and it had to be done in the living, not in the dying.

But what was the lesson?

If it wasn't the power of love's kiss, what was it?

While she ran and ran, she bargained and begged.

"I'll take his place. I'll die for him."

While she fought the power of the storm, her rage grew. It wasn't fair. She had forgiven him, loved him anyway. Wasn't that enough? What more was there for her to do?

The poor helpless children were frozen because of her stupid spell in some other life. They didn't deserve this. How could any kind of benevolent God let so many innocents suffer for her mistakes?

"Fuck you, Odin!" She cursed her God. But then she remembered something her grandmother had said once about life happening for you, not to you. *Could that have happened for the children, not to them?*

She remembered the pools of the deadno children.

"Oh my, Odin!" she exclaimed. "Are you protecting them? Protecting them from what I have done until I can undo it?"

She remembered the image in the magical glass of her lover carrying her sister up to the terrible Enfield beast. It was that horrifying image that infuriated her to the point of casting the spell responsible for all of this.

"What were you doing? Why did hold my sister like that? What information am I missing? What do I now know?" she screamed, certain the only answer that would come would be that of whipping and howling wind.

She looked down towards her feet, now covered by ice and snow, and there was Talby, like a gift out of nowhere.

She knew exactly what to do next.

"Take me to the beast," she told Talby. And he did.

Chapter Twenty-Six

IN TYNDRA:

As the pair approached the Ivy Wall, the other creatures parted ways to let her pass as if they knew her, as if they had planned this all along. Talby marched, head held high like the royal creature he was, into the center of the wall.

Azza walked through the thick wall shocked by the damage the storm had done to the massive structure. On the orange side, the ivy was frozen and falling down in splintered bits while the blue side seemed to be melting like wax. Only a few healthy vines remained leading to the center of the incredible and fantastic space. If tyme had allowed such luxury, she would have sat and marveled for hours, days, or weeks over the intricate masterpiece that her spell must have created.

"Wow, I am powerful," she whispered.

Talby mewed.

Azza had a plan. If she could convince the terrible beast to command all of his creatures to tear down the wall, then the ice from one side would cure the fires on the other. But how would she convince him to do her bidding? By promising to feed him and set him free, of course.

And what was the only way to get him to agree? Once the beast had eaten Azza, her spell would be gone, too, allowing him to break free of the prison in which she had encased him. She looked down at the blade and smiled. She would get the chance to take her lover's place after all.

The Witch Saccas cackled. That stupid girl Azza still thought she had a chance to undo the damage her curse had done. Unfortunately for her, there was one thing the witch knew that she didn't: the spell had only created the Ivy Wall. Azza could kill herself, and no amount of bargaining with princy-wincy Enfield would do her any good at all.

The spell was kept in place by the power of the Irminsul. The witch turned the half that remained between her handsthree turns to the right and three turns to the left. It felt good and strong, strong enough to hold until Azza was done sacrificing herself.

Shame though that when the witch laughed once more, she had no idea who stood behind the curtains watching her.

Chapter Twenty-Seven

WITH TALBY AS HER GUIDE, Azza made it to the heart of the Enfield's garden. The room was as large as the queen's castle and grander but in a solemn and mostly unrecognized way. Colored columns of swirling orange and blue vines, birthed from the branches of too many thick and woody plants to count, stretched from the floor to the ceiling and back again. Yet even the colors of the entangled leaves were hard to make out in the dim light.

Azza squinted her eyes with great effort, attempting to adjust them to the near darkness. She observed the bodies of the precious children who were so adored and missed, the young victims of the thieving creatures from both sides of the wall. Now that she knew how to look for them, who can say other than Odin how many petrified children she passed while she stepped through the tangled vines that surrounded her? None of the little ones seemed harmed in the slightest though, and she wondered what all these curious mutant creatures were doing as they stood still guarding each of their precious human bounties, camouflaged by all the colors behind them. She gazed upon the various creatures, animals with mixed compositions, some built with wrong heads for the wrong bodies, with mounting compassion and curiosity. If she had more tyme to waste, she might have catalogued them all. Maybe in the next life if one existed.

All of her most precious memories flashed in and out of her mind as she went to face himthis creature famous for his cruelty, his hideous face. Briefly, she considered that once she had thought the same of her belovedfamous for his cruelty. How ridiculous. Henrik had always been good. Funny how it had taken her so long to see it. Funny how the ideas she had about him had colored her experience of her tyme with him. Funny how it took losing him to know his truth.

She knew she should have been afraid in a moment like this, but that seemed silly to her right now.

Doing the right thing was never as scary as doing the wrong thing. *In comparison.*

She puffed out her chest and raised her head as she entered the central chamber.

Nothing could have prepared her for what she saw next.

Chapter Twenty-Eight

HERE, upon a great throne made of a ruddy orange marble, sat a creature she had no words to adequately describe. He sat like a man yet wore the face and the wings and claws of a terrible beast. His foxish head rested sadly on his chest as if he had sat there so long his muzzle had grown into his chest. His eyes glazed over with such apathy and distracted confusion that he might as well have been dead. Azza knew that lookthe look of frost heart, the look of burn heart, the look of lost love. His breathing remained slow and shallow as if the motion of taking another breath had become more painful to him than death.

Azza called the monster's name, and yet nothing moved.

Talby barked a high-pitched cry of pain.

In the far corner of the room was a beautiful maiden in a clear glass box surrounded by the golden statues of seven dwarves. It reminded her of a story, but she couldn't remember which one. All around the flawless coffin were beautiful offerings to the woman within. A shrine of gold pieces and fine lace displayed small hand carved figurines, dried flowers, letters upon letters upon more letters, and more baubles than she knew possible, even in the abundant kingdom of Ardnyt. She had never witnessed such devotion.

Dare she reach into the glass and pull the priceless veil, obviously stitched by a dedicated and loving hand, from the girl's eyes?

The veil and the material looked so familiar, just like…

It was another moment of *must*, because the *shouldn't* no longer mattered. She must know before she sacrificed herself to the beast to save her world.

But the veil. The material. She knew that material but couldn't remember why.

When she was finally brave enough to look at the maiden's face, Azza fell back and screamed. How was this possible? Everything she knew to be true crumbled into a thousand pieces on the floor, and she lost consciousness from the shock.

Chapter Twenty-Nine

IN ARDNYT:

"You bitch," the man accused, gathering his courage to attack her.

"You mean witch." Saccas stomped her foot and turned round to face him.

"No, I mean bitch." He spit at her beautiful face, one he had worshiped like a god's for so long."

She laughed. He did not.

"Funny thing," Kirnéh said, "about the curse you brainwashed me to say."

"Oh, yes. That. Ironic, isn't it? He's dead. Your other half. Henrik. You killed yourself."

"Well, sort of…"

"Does it hurt," the witch snarled, "to be half dead inside?"

"I don't know. But you might."

She paused, curious about what he was getting at, and observed him. He was handsome.

Shame she never took him to her bed. He could have put those big muscles to good use.

"Don't even look at me like that," he said. "I belong to Za."

Saccas snarled. "Pathetic. You two are so hopeless."

"Maybe. Or maybe not."

"What?"

"Like I was about to say, you should probably do a better job of casting spells."

"What...what do you mean?" she backed up, her mind reeling.

He laughed and loosened his grip on the arrow he held covertly behind his back and let it gather its speed.

He wanted to savor this moment. After all, it had been a while since he had killed a witch. Or a giant. Or a magical dragon.

It didn't take long for the witch to realize her error. *"From me back on to you, my arrow take flight and might it strike true. On cursed winds, through bondage vinemark pain's truest source, the source of tyme."*

"You and your evil plots," he vowed with absolute certainty, "not my curious little Za, are the true source of this existence called tyme."

He released the cursed arrow, and it struck the evil sorceress straight through her black, empty heart.

Chapter Thirty

IN THE WALL:

Eventually, Azza woke and crawled with crippling misery, unbearable guilt, and a thousand steaming tears to soak the monster's feet.

"Forgive me, Prince Enfield, for what I have done. I didn't know. I didn't know you loved her, that you loved anything."

Still the beast sat, lost in a thousand prisons made of sorrow far more inescapable than the vines of ivy that actually kept him captive. There was no chance of escape for him, monster or no. He tried to respond but couldn't; his lips just barely formed the terrible word "love".

Azza looked him up and down, trembling with fear. But then she remembered she had been deceived by looks more than once in the recent past.

This tyme, she closed her eyes and let her heart show her the truth of the hideous creature in front of her. Less fearful by the moment, she touched his face and jumped back in shock. His skin was lovely. The lines of his face were perfect. His cheekbones were high and fine and his forehead fair and regal. His locks gold, soft and full, bounced with glory. Where her eyes had shown her menacing wings, putrid claws, and dripping fangs, her heart showed the grace of his perfect body beneath the witch's spell. This man was a god in physical form, finer than Odin, most likely.

Her tears fell even faster, for she knew this fine and physically flawless prince had loved her sisterthe one who lay in the coffin of glasswith all his heart, the same heart famous for loving the children of his barren land. *The children!*

"You saved them," she whispered. "You trapped them so the storm wouldn't harm them. You loved her, loved the children. You never ate her, and your beasts never ate them. You were trying…."

He moved so slightly she questioned if she had imagined it at first.

"You were trying," she slowly whispered.

"To wed her," he said, the words so soft and low and coated with layers of eternal misery that Azza rather she died than hear him utter one more syllable.

Azza wept, and he wept with her.

"When she saw my terrible face…"

"She went into shock…"

"And there she remains. I have her, yet I cannot have her. That has been the most terrible part of my prison. I must look upon what I cannot have every moment of tyme, and I am helpless to change things."

"I did this." Azza scrambled to her feet and stumbled back.

"No, the Witch Saccas did this."

"It is unforgivable."

"No. I forgive you, Za. You're but a pawn in that witch's scheming ways of becoming Queen. And this tyme King, too."

"No! My king was the witch? How didn't I realize the truth? It's just not possible. I loved him, and he was kind and fair unlike her! That witch."

"Actually, to be fair, Za, I did this. If only I had wed that ugly heathen, your sister would be free, and the glory of the past memories would still belong to the once happy children and people of these lands."

"No."

"Yes. And now you see my ivy is dying, and so I am dying. I cannot set things straight and release the past by allowing your beautiful sister to go free."

"Why hasn't Odin done something to help us?"

"Don't you know your father's ways better than that, Za?" he asked. The wise, terribly depressed prince would have smiled had he not forgotten how. "Oh Odin, I miss her lovely smile. How do I get her back?" He wept briefly before resuming his prior slumped position as his words seemed to crawl back up inside his mouth to die a terrible, silent death.

"Return to me, Prince," Za said. "Where is Odin now? Why won't he help us? Damn him!"

It took a while, but eventually the Enfield gathered the energy to move his mouth again. "No more curses out of you, little one. And who says He hasn't helped us? You made it here to see the real me, to see that your sister lived, didn't you? Perhaps you are still asking the wrong questions of your God and making demands on love where there should be no such things as demands? "

Azza looked at Talby, wondering if perhaps he was a message from Odin.

"Besides, answering you directly is not Odin's way, really. One can only learn a lesson by learning it, don't you think? If He carries us too far, we will have to learn it another way, and all of this tyme will have been wasted."

Azza knew something about wasting tyme. While she thought about the significance of that, she asked, "What, pray tell, is the lesson?"

"If only it were that easy." The beast looked at the ivy on the ground, disease spreading quickly from one frond of the ivy to the next.

"What if I…" Azza's wheels were spinning now. "Can I give you my beauty? Then you can wake Urtha and escape. At least the two of you shall be free."

"You wouldn't do that. Such a sacrifice"

"Of course I would."

"But the witch took your lover. Why would you wish that I get to have mine?"

"First of all, she's my sister. I love her. And, oddly enough, I think I love you now, too."

"Thank you. But I'm"

"Ugly. So freaking what?" And only on the outside. That isn't who you are. Who you are on the inside is the real you. Only the heart can see the truth. The eyes lie and make the image of what the brain tells us to see. If we get stuck in our head, we are as good as dead." She giggled, the irony too absurd to ignore. "But if we can just find a way to love in our hearts, then we are truly free to see with clear eyes and, eventually, a clear mind."

The beast realized before Azza did that she was getting close to finding the answer she sought. In fact, he couldn't be sure, but somehow he knew Odin was standing right behind them in observance of this moment in tyme.

"Besides, just because I'm hurting"

The prince choked. Now he knew what the lesson was. But did Azza?

Azza was starting to figure it out, too. She said it again for clarity. "That just because I'm hurting doesn't mean…"

The prince smiled. For the first tyme in eons, he smiled.

Azza didn't need to finish her sentence now. She understood. It had to come to this or she wouldn't have ever understood. They both understood.

She placed her hands on the monster's terrible face, but this tyme she kept her eyes open and only allowed her heart to show her the way *in comparison*. Only then did her mind see him as clearly as her heart.

"My pain need not be your pain. The purpose of my pain was to teach me how to keep you from having to experience it, not to show me how to spread it to you to make mine less. That would only make... Oh my Odin, that would only make my suffering more, not less."

"I see."

"I see," she said. "Yes, finally I see." *In comparison.*

The Enfield laughed, or howled or barked depending on which ears you listened with. However, if you listened with your heart, it was a delightful full-bodied laugh of merry kings and fertile queens.

Tears streaming down her face, Za, both forwards and backwards as Azza, stood and bowed her head. With the clarity of her heart, she prayed a special prayer. Or spell if you preferred...

"Holy Father, Holy Mother, all that is good and full of grace, I take my beauty and make it his. For I can only give those things which I already own. And I can only truly own that which I freely give. And this, the beauty of my outer self and the inner lesson that I have learned on this journey towards truth *in comparison*. I offer it freely as retribution for my crimes, the same crimes I said were done unto me but actually were done by me against this man, against You my Holy Father and Holy Mother, against my sister, against all my sisters, against all the goodness of the snow globe."

A voice of perfectly silent wisdom infused the room, and

sparkles filled the air whilst a breeze almost as subtle as a kiss passed Azza's cheek.

"But most of all, Father Odin and Mother Nido, against myself."

Azza waved her hand across her chest to work her magic, and just before she sealed the pact to swap her lovely face with that of the cursed prince, Kirnéh crashed through the door carrying the body of the Witch Saccas. He blew his favorite girl, the youngest but probably most interesting of all her sisters, love's first kiss and stunned her with such force she fell back at just the right tyme.

Or was it time?

And, of course, the clever soldier tossed the witch's dead body into the air at just the right tyme to take Azza's place. Just like someone somewhere in another universe had written it in a fairytale, the unconditional love's spell worked its magic perfectly.

Like it always did.

Like it always has.

Like it always does.

Like it always will.

Because, after all, everyone, especially those who live in snow globes, knows that true love, the kind without any conditions or rules, is always the answer. Even though it doesn't always seem to be at first glance, love's first kiss is the most powerful of all possible magic, or prayers, or spells if you preferred.

Every single tyme.

And every time, too.

And because fair is fair, after all…

The terrible witch was not only as good as dead but ugly once more.

The prince, no longer a hideous beast, was fine and handsome.

Za (as Azza) and Enhrik (as Kirnéh) embraced a million embraces all at once.

A golden silence in the back of the room laughed the sweetest laugh that ever laughed in perfect, soundless observance of this magical moment in tyme just before it blew them all one more whisper of love's first kiss, a kiss of unconditional love that cannot ever falter or forsake.

The glass box shattered whilst the maiden within it stood up ready to finish the vows she had been saying just a short time before. The bride, eldest and most beautiful of the Norns, Urtha, pulled back her veil, the one her sweet little sister Za had made for her by hand, and wondered why she felt so darn sleepy.

Best of all, suddenly remembering a lost memory so funny, wonderful, and perfect, a thousand children across as many worlds laughed simultaneously causing all that had ever been good to shake with joy.

How odd that they had forgotten something so darn funny. Silly things, memories. It's funny how they worked, almost like a magical Norn weaved them to be better than the event that had created them in the first place. Oh well.

Did it really matter how the memories came back to the children?

Probably not. But maybe so.

Who, other than Odin, could have possibly known?

Epilogue

AS QUICKLY AS the youngest of the Norns had fallen into a trance during her journey into tyme, the fickle little Za awoke from it. It seemed like such a silly little waste of her time now that she had better things to do. Like…hanging out with her demigod in this realm to set things straight…and maybe even forgive, should he be deserving of her pardon.

Oh who was she kidding? She always forgave that delicious young man with those buttery lips made from the same miracles that had created the stars. Or was it that he was always forgiving her and her ways? Not surprisingly, she was too distracted by the idea of finding him to remember who would make the first apology.

But did that even matter? Probably not, she decided.

Besides, she had a sister to try to understand better. She loved her three sisters more than all the constellations in the sky, moon, and suns combined; she always had.

They had so many interesting lessons to teach her.

Especially Urtha, the most gorgeous of the Norns, who loved the horrific looking Enfield by simply looking past the illusion of his ghastly external appearance and focusing on his kind heart, inner valor, and love for children instead.

That was true love, surely.

Oh, but in comparison, did Za have true love or just buttery lips to nibble upon? Maybe she needed to ask the question so the answer would come fumbling towards her as it always did.

She said it out loud, twice. "What makes a love true love? How can I tell the difference? And do I really have to be willing to love the face of a beast to know my affection is real?"

The idea was absurd, for certain.

Loving a beast was not for her, she decided. Maybe Urtha was big enough for such grand stupidity but not Za.

She was just too fickle to love a beast's face for what was underneath it. Or was she? She couldn't be sure anymore. The memory of the idea seemed so lovely to her at the same time that it seemed so terrible. Perhaps that was Urtha's fault now that she was back at weaving memory in a more favorable light.

Anyway… such a lovely story the tale would make. Probably one of the best fairytales of all times, in fact. Za did love her fairytales, after all. Of course she did. She had written them all, every single one from the beginning of time, including her journey into tyme.

The beauty and the beast. Ah! *Imagine that*, Za thought. Such a great title for spinning an unforgettable story to pass down to the humans all so infatuated with the idea of love's first kiss. Such a whim, that idea. Instantly, the passion to commit the story to the written page consumed her usually flittering desires, and she forgot all about her annoyance with Odin, the boss of everything in her universe who could have just as easily answered her question in the first place.

But maybe not?

Maybe the journey to find her own answer to her own question was the destination, after all. Well, screw Him and His divine brilliance. Ugh! Even she had to admit He was right. But it would be a while before she said it out loud to anyone other than a little lamb who belonged to a girl name Mary.

Once done perfecting the details of her newest story, she would have to whisper a sweet, yet deliciously evil version of it in the ears of the Brothers Grimmthose goons who thought they invented all the stories they were so famous for writing. Fools! One day, they would learn the truth. But until then…

It was, after all, such a beautiful ideafinding the gift of light in the darkest of places. *In comparison.*

The more she thought about it, the more Za realized that maybe poverty gave abundance its value, darkness clarified the light, sadness brought forth the possibility of joy, and maybe even the terrible face of a beast was what made the sweetest and most handsome of faces so wonderful to look upon. For opposites were just both flip sides of the same coin, and one side of the coin was simply invisible without the other to offer it definition by contrast. *In comparison.*

Is that what "as above, so below" really meant?

After so much thinking, her brain hurt, and she decided to leave that question where she had asked it for a little while.

Then, because it was the right thing to do, after all, she set the snow globe upright and let all the things settle back where they might. Many of the good things landed on the side that had once only held what she had previously considered to be bad, and bad things on the side that had once only held the things she had considered to be good. She giggled at the grand irony of life.

Just to be certain things stayed so perfectly mixed up, she took the cracked stick out of the middle of the globe and threw it away forever. It was useless to her now that she was absolutely certain the letters written on it, and more importantly their meanings, were the same whether she used them forward or backward. In T-Y-N-D-R-A, in the heart of Odin's heart, in the only place that matteredthe center of all things good and small that have ever matteredthere is where Tyndra turns to Ardnyt.

She put the snow globe back in her pocket and yawned, feeling more and more distracted by the moment. And as she opened her tomb, such a creepy and bug-infested place it suddenly seemed, she smiled as wide as her face would allow and looked out onto the light of day. The same light she would have never noticed were it not for the darkness of the tomb.

It was, after all, hardly noon…with plenty of time, if not tyme, left to spare for her next, and maybe even more interesting, adventure.

Books in the Norn Novella Series

About the Author

A. Nicky Hjort is originally from the greater Dallas-Fort Worth area of Texas. She writes stories that cross multiple genre lines, from paranormal romance to Sci-Fi thrillers and back again. And in some subtle way, all of her manuscripts are connected, with their purpose to explore all facets of love and what it has to teach us. Her journey into writing began with her clinical background as a medical doctor when she wrote her first fictional short story about medicine. She hasn't stopped writing since.

Facebook author page:
https://www.facebook.com/Author.A.N.Hjort
Twitter: @A_NickyHjort
Website: www.anickyhjortbooks.com
Blog: www.ANickyHjortBooks.com
Instagram: https://www.instagram.com/nickyhjort

Also by A. NICKY HJORT

https://www.amazon.com/A.-Nicky-Hjort/e/B01M30LVVM/

Sinister Bouquet: Awakening - Devyn Mitchell has a choice… listen to the voice of her unborn baby – or die- again. After a near death experience, Doctor Devyn Mitchell finds herself not only mysteriously pregnant but able to communicate with her fetus. She has two choices: give in to total madness or surrender to her new reality, which just may be the only way she and her family will survive the obsessions of the Homeless Hunter's mind.

A true paranormal romantic thriller, A Sinister Bouquet: Awakening, the first of the Sinister Series, will take you right to the edge of what you know to be possible and then drop you in a place so dark, so terrifying, that the only passageway out is through the blinding light of awakening. (MA18+ for graphic sexual and violent content)

The City Series - A futuristic Sci-fi at its best! Kidnapped and genetically altered, Isla-Jane-53 lives in a world where Ink enhanced with bacteria is used for tattooing warriors in a living video game. One of the inhabitants of The City, she is forced to her battle her fellow man, natural disasters, and vicious creatures, all for the pleasure of hidden viewers she has no idea exist. A fantastic trilogy, The City Series will thrill and excite in ways you cannot imagine. Look for book 1 – The Jane harvest, spring of 2017!

Also from the Lavish family

Irrevocable Series
Samantha Jacobey
http://myBook.to/TheIrrevocableSeries

The end of the world is coming, or so they say, and that puts Bailey Dewitt on a crash course with Armageddon. Orphaned, she and her young brothers find themselves living with their renegade uncle as part of a group of survivalists. She struggles against them, searching for a way to escape, but every discovery only terrifies her more.

For Caleb Cross, the Ranch is a way of life. The members of their group are family, and none should come between them. Smitten from the moment he met Bailey, his choices are no longer easy, his path no longer clear. He wants to welcome her and the twins into their fold and hopes his kin will agree.

But the elders who lead them aren't interested in the trouble-some girl. They are plotting for the time they will be rid of her and expect Caleb to go along with their plans - he is after all one of them.

At first, Bailey resists Caleb's charms, but soon must admit that she desperately needs a friend. She has no intention of anything more, but when the elders make their move, she is forced to trust him with her very life.

They both have hard lessons to learn. Relationships built on secrets and lies don't come with guarantees. When the world falls apart around them, some things are Irrevocable.

Rosinanti Series
Kevin J. Kessler
http://myBook.to/RosinantiSeries

The Rosinanti Dragons are no more. Since their extinction nearly one thousand years ago these primal powerhouses have fallen into the obscurity of history's forgotten lore. In that time, humans have come to dominate the world of Terra, peacefully ignorant to one horrifying truth: ancient evil stirs around them, waiting to reclaim its lost world.

For Valentean Burai, animus warrior of the kingdom of Kack-ritta, the details surrounding humanity's victory over the Rosinanti are more than just a history lesson. The long-buried mysteries of this archaic conflict may hold the answers that he has so desperately sought regarding his own past.

As the awful truth of the Rosinanti's supposed demise comes to light, Valentean must stand together with Seraphina, a magically gifted princess, to embark upon a mission to maintain order and light throughout Terra. Only together can these two lifelong friends face down the resurgence of the Rosinanti legacy and combat the greatest threat their world has ever known.

www.ingramcontent.com/pod-product-compliance
Lightning Source LLC
Chambersburg PA
CBHW051244170626
46809CB00004B/1476

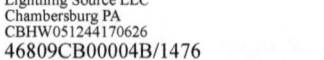